DIAMOND CHARM

DIAMOND CHARM

JENNY OLDFIELD

Illustrated by
Paul Hunt

**Hodder
Children's
Books**

a division of Hodder Headline Limited

For Bex

First published in Great Britain in 2002
by Hodder Children's Books

10 9 8 7 6 5 4 3 2 1

A Catalogue record for this book is available from the British
Library

ISBN 0 340 84353 5

Typeset by Avon Dataset Ltd, Bidford-on-Avon, Warks

Printed and bound in Great Britain by
The Guernsey Press Co. Ltd, Channel Isles

Hodder Children's Books
a division of Hodder Headline Limited
338 Euston Road
London NW1 3BH

1

'Say what you like, Taryn West is one damaged kid!'
Sandy Scott ended the conversation with her son,
Matt, on an emphatic note. She grabbed her car
key and strode out of the house.

Kirstie Scott left off eating her blueberry waffle
to listen hard. This had been a scorching exchange
between her brother and mom, and one which Matt
had definitely lost.

'How come we're not askin' this girl's folks
to pay for her stay with us?' he'd demanded
as Kirstie had dragged herself sleepily downstairs.
Breakfast was already on the table and their
mom was in her smart town shirt and new jeans,

pulling on her best cowboy boots.

'Because!' Sandy had replied.

'What kind of answer is that?' Matt had been frowning as he poured himself coffee.

'It's the only kind of answer you're gonna get.'

'Yeah, but what sense does it make? Here we are, in high season, with all the cabins fully booked way through to the end of August. And what d'you do? Why, you offer a place to an eleven-year-old girl and don't charge her a single cent!'

'Yeah,' Sandy had doggedly agreed. 'Not only that, I open up our own house for her. She'll be using the spare bedroom overlooking the corral.'

'Huh?' Matt had been speechless at this.

'Hey, how come you didn't say anythin'?' Kirstie had chipped in. Having a live-in guest at Half-Moon Ranch certainly was a little out of the ordinary.

'Because!' Her mum had stayed tight-lipped. 'Oh and by the way, I know you two will both be good hosts to our visitor. Kirstie, you can show her around the ranch later this morning, and Matt, you choose her a good pony, keepin' in mind that Taryn is new to horse-riding.'

Matt had sniffed and muttered, 'Oh, great!' under his breath. 'Not only does the kid stay free, she gets to spoil one of our valuable quarter-horses!'

Sandy had made one more effort to make him look beyond the question of payment. 'Listen Matt, I'm breakin' my own strict rule here, and don't think I don't know it. And sure we're strugglin' like usual to pay the bills and keep our heads above water. But trust me, Taryn West is a special case!'

Stubborn Matt had kept right on grumbling while Kirstie had flipped a hot waffle out of the machine on to her plate and drowned it in blueberry syrup. The atmosphere stayed tense, until in the end, Sandy had made her 'damaged kid' remark and walked out.

'Good job, Matt!' Kirstie teased. 'Mom sure appreciated your input!'

Lifting his stetson from the coat-hook by the door, he dusted it down. 'She calls herself a hard-headed business woman, yet she offers a free vacation, all because she feels sorry for what this kid is goin' through.'

'What *is* she goin' through?' Kirstie felt more and more intrigued. Personally, she'd never heard the name Taryn West before. There again, maybe she had. It rang a few distant bells, but nothing that she could call to mind.

Prodding Matt for more information, but receiving only grunts by way of reply, Kirstie saved up the mystery to pass on to her best friend, Lisa Goodman, when she arrived in an hour's time.

'Sure you know who Taryn West is!' Lisa swung one leg over the corral fence to sit alongside Kirstie. 'The whole of Colorado has heard of the Wests!'

'I do? They have?' Kirstie thought hard. 'Where do they live?'

'In Marlowe County, dumbo! They stay right on the edge of town, out near the county line.'

'Yeah, right.' Kirstie watched Ben, Matt and Karina get guests into the saddle for the morning trail-ride. A heavy guy from Texas had to be practically winched on to Crazy Horse, his poor mount for the week. Other visitors sat nervously in the deep leather saddles while their bored ponies semi-snoozed. 'But I never saw Taryn West at inter-school sports events,' she pointed out. At eleven years old, Taryn was only two years junior to Lisa and herself.

'No, you wouldn't. Her parents have home-schooled her since she was five.'

'Huh.' Kirstie's shrug showed that she didn't approve. Even though she lived way out of town herself and had to make a tough daily journey to get to school, no way would she go for home schooling. 'Sounds pretty lonely to me,' she commented.

'That was the point about the Wests when they hit the headlines,' Lisa told her. 'Everyone said they'd been living in their own little world, shunning contact with reality. It was one of the reasons they gave for the weird thing that happened to them.'

Kirstie dragged her gaze away from the perspiring Texan. She saw that her livewire friend was fizzing over with gossip. 'OK, give me the lowdown,' she grinned.

'I still wanna know what planet you're livin' on!' Lisa teased. 'The stuff was in all the newspapers a couple of months back, around late May.'

'Hey, Lisa!' Matt interrupted as he walked by. He made as if to topple her off the fence backwards, then quickly pulled her back to safety.

'Don't do that!' she squealed. 'I'm tryin' to have a serious conversation here!'

'Yeah, yeah. Quit the small talk and open the corral gate, would ya! Karina's group is rarin' to go!'

'Tell you later!' Lisa muttered as she sprang from the fence and landed on the dusty ground. Quickly she wove between the horses and their riders to open the wide metal gate and set the bunch of advanced riders on their way.

'You girls wanna ride over to Renegade with me and pick up a new mare?' Matt asked Kirstie.

'You bet! – Oh jeez, no! I guess I'd better hang out until Mom gets back from town with Taryn.' Kirstie remembered her promise to show the newcomer around.

'Are you sure about that?' Through the dust and scuffle of the departing horses, Matt enjoyed twisting the knife a little. 'This is a real nice mare – registered quarter-horse named Diamond Charm. We're renting her for the rest of the summer season from Dwight Lebowski at the Triple X. You'll fall for her the second you set eyes on her!'

'Thanks, Matt,' Kirstie sighed. Then she turned to Lisa with a generous offer. 'You go! He'll need some help loading the trailer and driving the mare home.'

Her friend grabbed the chance with, 'You bet!' and a sprint towards the silver truck.

In less than five minutes, Matt had finished his work in the corral and joined Lisa to set off on the forty-mile journey north to Renegade.

Kirstie clicked her tongue in a tutting sound, then set about clearing up the corral after the departure of the last trail-riders. The head wrangler, Ben Marsh, had given her a sympathetic nod and an invitation to join them. 'Later, huh?' She'd nodded, and now she was scooping poop on to a wide shovel and tipping it into the truck before Hadley Crane drove it off to the manure heap behind the Dump.

Like, very glamorous! she muttered to herself. But, sleeves rolled up and baseball cap pulled low to shade her face from the rising sun, she worked on through the morning. First clearing the corral, then untying spare lead-ropes from the thick poles and hanging them in a set position from the hooks in the tack-room, she took a broom and, in amongst the smell of dusty saddle pads and old leather, she set about sweeping the tack-room floor.

'Sorry, Cornbread!' she murmured as she disturbed the sleeping kitten.

The young yellow cat vacated his shady corner and strolled outside into the bright sun. Then Hadley poked his head around the adjoining office door. 'Phone call for the boss!' he called.

'Not here!' Kirstie yelled back. The dust was getting to her and making her cough.

The old man grunted. 'When will she be back?'

Kirstie looked at her watch. 'Soon, I guess.' Then, hearing the rumble of a Jeep engine coming down the hill, she peered through the window. 'Right now, in fact!'

The retired wrangler disappeared to relay her message, while Kirstie went outside to dust herself down. Her reflection in the tack-room window showed a dishevelled, tall girl with a ponytail of golden-blonde hair trapped beneath a faded denim cap. She groaned, dusted some more, then sneezed.

Meanwhile, Sandy Scott's Jeep pulled up in the yard.

Aaatchoo! Kirstie's sneeze sent Cornbread skedaddling across the corral. He dipped under the fence and sought refuge under the parked Jeep.

Kirstie watched the passenger door open. She saw her mom come round and hold it wide. Slowly, a thin, dark-haired girl climbed down. She was dressed in jeans that looked too big and a loose blue plaid shirt. Her short hair was styled way too young, as if scissors had sliced it off carelessly at chin level, and been equally haphazard with heavy bangs across her forehead. Beneath the hair, her brown eyes were cast down towards the ground.

'Kirstie, come and take Taryn's bag!' Sandy said brightly. 'It's in the back of the car.'

So Kirstie took a deep breath, saying a cheery hi

as she crossed the yard and lifted out the light bag.

Taryn didn't raise her gaze, but her pale face went red with embarrassment. She reacted slowly to Sandy's invitation to come inside.

'Good journey?' Kirstie asked, trying to break the ice.

The girl shrugged.

'How was the traffic in Marlowe County?'

Another shrug.

'Hadley said it was crazy yesterday afternoon when he was in town. Hadley used to be head wrangler here until he retired. Now Ben Marsh has taken over. You'll get to meet him over lunch maybe. And Karina Cooper – she organises the kids' program for the summer. I guess she'll be the one who allocates you a horse.'

Still silence from their new guest.

Kirstie put her bag down on the porch and prattled on. 'Mom says you're new to horse-riding, but it doesn't matter in the least. At Half-Moon Ranch we have horses to suit all abilities, including beginners.' Jeez, she was starting to sound like the ranch brochure!

'Come right on in, Taryn, and let me show you your room.' Sandy took over, much to Kirstie's relief.

She watched her mom take the visitor upstairs, wondering how on earth they were going to handle things. Taryn had already made it clear that she wasn't pleased to be here. In fact, she showed no reaction at all, not even a flicker of interest in the layout of the corral and tack-room, nor in the quaint, frontier style of the old log ranch house.

I wonder how long she's gonna stay? Kirstie thought. Then she gave herself a shake. That was a mean question of which she was ashamed. Better take up the bag and help Taryn settle in, act like she was glad to have someone new and round about her own age in the house.

'So this is the closet for your clothes, and you'll find the bathroom down the corridor, first on your left,' Sandy was saying.

Taryn trailed Kirstie's mom from room to room like a limp rag doll. When they came back into the bedroom, Kirstie was about to unzip the crumpled hold-all and help unpack.

'Don't do that!' Taryn said sharply – the first words she'd uttered since she'd arrived.

Kirstie drew quickly back. *OK, OK, don't jump down my throat!*

Sandy threw her a rapid glance. 'So, we'll leave you to arrange your things how you want,' she told

Taryn. 'Lunch is at twelve-thirty, but come down when you're ready.'

They made their exit and headed for the kitchen.

Before Kirstie could speak, Sandy raised both hands. 'Don't say anything!' she warned in a low voice. 'These walls aren't soundproof, remember!'

'But I need to know!' Kirstie protested. 'What's the mystery here? Why have you invited her?'

'Not now – later!' her mom insisted. 'In fact, the less you know, the better. The idea is for the poor kid to escape her past, at least for a week or two. She needs some space, without people looking at her and whispering behind her back. She's had enough of that these last few weeks, I'll bet!'

'Yeah, but if I acted that way, I'd be grounded!' Kirstie couldn't get over the sullen, silent air of boredom that the kid gave off. Her thin face looked as though it never cracked into a smile, and she didn't give eye contact. It was as if you didn't exist, unless you touched her precious bag and then she bawled you out!

'OK, I'll tell you the one thing that perhaps you ought to know,' Sandy conceded, setting plates and cutlery on the kitchen table.

From upstairs, the sound of their guest's footsteps

treading softly across the bedroom floor filtered down.

'Taryn just lost her mom,' Sandy confided.

Kirstie started. 'How d'you mean, "lost"?'

'Mariah West went missing. The police suspect that she's dead, but no one knows for sure.'

'Jeez!' Kirstie breathed out slowly. 'Poor kid!'

'Yeah, like you say, poor kid! She's an only child, and according to what folks say, she doesn't have friends or family to turn to.'

'What about her dad?' Kirstie jumped in with the obvious question.

Sandy's eyes narrowed and she hesitated. 'Let's just say that Sean West is having a hard time himself right now.'

A door opening and shutting on the landing let them know that the visitor was on her way down. Sandy quickly changed tack. 'Go ring the bell for lunch,' she told Kirstie. 'And remember, don't pry. Taryn's been through enough already.'

Though Kirstie made a resolution not to ask any more questions, she couldn't help but stare at Taryn through lunch when she thought her visitor wasn't looking.

How did it feel to have your mom go missing, she

wondered. One moment she was there doing all the things moms did, then next thing you knew, she'd vanished. It must make your whole world fall apart. Kirstie studied the kid's pale, expressionless face, her blank, empty eyes. Eleven was young. You still really needed your mom. Kirstie had been around that age when both her grandparents had died, and that had been hard to take. But her actual mom!

Sandy dished out pizza to a hungry crew, including Karina, Ben and Hadley. Amidst the clash of plates and the buzz of conversation, Taryn sat in silent misery. She took a slice of pizza, chewed a couple of mouthfuls, then stared into space. Then, when Karina tried to tell her about the fun rodeo planned for the end of the week, Taryn blanked her.

'I'll catch you later,' Karina said, reaching for her hat and going to find a more responsive audience amongst the bunch of kids crowding round the corral.

'Hey, I'll go bring Skylark in from Red Fox Meadow!' Ben got up to follow Karina. 'She's a nice little bay mare to start you ridin',' he told Taryn.

But Taryn stared through him without blinking, like she hadn't even heard.

*   *   *

'You'd swear she was deaf!' Kirstie whispered in Lisa's ear. Her friend had just got back – too late for lunch and sweating in the heat of the midday sun. 'I'm trying my hardest to be nice, but I tell you, it ain't easy!'

Lisa downed a can of cold Coke, then helped Matt to lower the trailer ramp. Inside, the stamp and rattle of a horse's hooves told Kirstie that their mission to the Triple X had been successful.

She'd seen this twenty times or more – the arrival of a new addition to the Half-Moon Ranch ramuda. Yet it still gave Kirstie the biggest buzz.

The wary horse would emerge in an agitated state, sweating down his flanks and rolling his eyes wildly to suck in his new surroundings. Were there mountain lions or bears ready to pounce? Were there allies in the shape of other horses? Did these humans who had shut him in a dark box mean him harm? He would be on the end of a lead-rope, pulling back, ready to rear.

And sure enough, the clattering of hooves as Matt went into the trailer to untie the new mare told Kirstie and the other onlookers that Diamond Charm was worked up. They heard a high whinny and Matt's voice trying to soothe her with, 'Easy, girl, no one's gonna hurt you!'

'She's a beauty!' Lisa promised. 'Named after her father, Silver Charm, the most valuable stud this side of Marlowe County.'

'Did she load easy?' Kirstie wanted to know, craning for a better view. Behind her, half a dozen guests had wandered down from their cabins to spectate, including two small brothers, sons of the heavy Texan named Earl Liston.

'She loaded like a dream,' Lisa answered. 'But it's hot in there and we had trouble with the traffic in San Luis. There's no wonder she's a little wired up!'

'Stand clear!' Matt warned.

Out of the corner of her eye, Kirstie caught sight of Taryn standing with Sandy on the house porch. She turned away to make sure that the Liston boys were at a safe distance, then when she glanced up again, noticed that Taryn had drifted closer. *Hmm, that's a good sign!* she thought.

'Here we come!' Matt's announcement brought him stepping on to the ramp with Diamond Charm pressing against his shoulder. The first thing Kirstie noted was the perfect, pure white diamond on the mare's forehead. The face was small and pretty, the eyes wide-set, the nostrils flared. Then there was her colour – a deep coppery sorrel which shone in the sun.

Yeah, a real beauty! Kirstie thought.

Matt struggled to keep Diamond Charm behind him as he descended the ramp, lead-rope in hand. The mare pushed forward, revealing a long, graceful neck and the usual athletic body of the true quarter-horse. Her mane and tail were thick and long, and there were no other markings except the white diamond on her entire coat.

As the mare skittered sideways off the end of the ramp, Kirstie saw Taryn take up position by the cab of the trailer. There was a new look on her face

that had transformed her from rag doll to an alert, alive, normal eleven-year-old. Her blank eyes had gathered depth and sparkle, there was a hint of colour in her white face.

'What d'you think?' Matt was asking the experts, Sandy and Ben.

'Real nice,' came the verdict from the young head wrangler. 'Good conformation, sound feet.'

'How about her temperament?' Sandy asked, getting close enough to handle the still fidgety mare. She ran both hands up Diamond Charm's neck, then down and under her belly, testing out the horse's sensitive areas with calm, soothing hands.

'We're not sure yet,' Matt answered. 'Lebowski reckons she's been a good roper and cutter this spring, though last fall his head wrangler had a little trouble with her. They say it's because she lost her mother when she was six weeks old. They had to hand rear her after that, and it can do bad things to a horse's temperament.'

'Well, let's hope she doesn't turn mean on us again.' Sandy's examination of the mare seemed to have had a calming effect, and the small crowd's interest was beginning to wane.

As people drifted off to prepare for the afternoon's trail-ride and Matt led Diamond Charm gently towards the row stalls, Kirstie and Lisa made their way to join Taryn.

'What d'you think?' Lisa urged the shy guest.

All she had to say was 'neat' or 'cool' – just the slightest show of the enthusiasm that Kirstie had seen in her eyes.

But no. The blankness came back, and the limp, listless body language. After her one positive moment, Taryn shrank away. She turned with a shake of her head, drifting back towards the house.

'How d'you like that?' Lisa hissed. Then, more kindly with a sigh, 'I guess that's what happens when your mom disappears!'

2

Kirstie's mom had said, 'Don't pry' when Taryn first arrived at the ranch. But this was easier said than done.

For a start, there were the few solid facts that made Taryn West more interesting than their average guest. Here was a kid whose mom had simply vanished into thin air, who had lived a secluded, almost secret life through all of her eleven years. And from what Sandy had told Matt, these experiences had left her severely damaged.

Then there were glimpses that Lisa had added – the hint that the Wests' history had been splashed over the newspapers and the feeling that there was something truly shocking about Mariah West's disappearance.

Plus – and this was new since last night – Kirstie had discovered the reason why Taryn had yelled at her for trying to unzip her bag.

'Hey honey, would you take these fresh towels up to Taryn's room and store them in her closet?' Sandy had asked while their guest was taking a shower in the bathroom late on Monday evening.

Kirstie had carried up the small pile of towels as asked. She'd opened the closet door, expecting to see Taryn's belongings – T-shirts, shirts, trousers, maybe a couple of skirts or dresses. But to her surprise she'd found only one faded green plaid shirt and a beat-up pair of trainers. No wonder the bag had been so light! But how come Taryn had come on a visit with so few possessions?

A second, closer look had revealed a small pile of what looked like hand-made birthday cards tied with a yellow ribbon. Kirstie had lifted the corner of the top card and read the message – 'To darling Taryn on her eleventh birthday, With love from Mommy and Daddy'. A quick count had revealed a total of eleven cards – one for each year, which the girl had tied up into this precious bundle and brought with her.

No clothes but a stack of birthday cards. Hot with embarrassment, Kirstie had closed the closet door and retreated downstairs.

'Anything the matter?' Sandy had asked.

Kirstie had mumbled something about Taryn not bringing many spare clothes, and her mom had nodded thoughtfully.

'Don't say anything!' Kirstie had jumped ahead. 'If we focus attention on it by offering to lend her fresh shirts etcetera, it might only make it worse!'

'Gotcha,' Sandy said quietly. Then she'd smiled sadly at her own daughter and came out with the by now usual 'poor kid'.

But to Kirstie, early next morning, the 'poor kid' syndrome had already turned to 'this kid is driving me nuts'!

Trying to get Taryn to talk was like squeezing blood from a stone. A grunt was the most Kirstie could expect from questions such as 'Who's your favourite popstar?' or 'What's your best subject and what's your worst?'

'My best subject is Science!' Kirstie had rattled on. It was breakfast time, and once more Taryn was pushing the food around her plate with her fork. 'Especially animal biology. I hope to go to college and study to be a vet, like Matt. That's if I don't go for the rodeo rider option, like Karina. And Mom's boyfriend, Brad, was runner-up in the national reining championship. That'd be a neat career choice for anyone who's into horses, don't you think?'

Taryn shrugged and stood up, tugging awkwardly at the hem of the same blue shirt that she'd worn the day before.

'OK, you ready to come and find Karina?' Kirstie took a deep breath. It was only eight o'clock and her cheeriness was already wearing pretty thin.

'What for?' Taryn frowned.

'To get you a saddle and meet Skylark. She's gonna be your horse, remember!'

The frown deepened. 'Do I have to?'

'Huh?' Kirstie couldn't make out what the question meant.

'Do I have to go riding while I'm here?' Taryn muttered.

Kirstie stared hard, and just managed to stop her jaw from dropping. 'Well, yeah. Riding is what you do when you come to a ranch, I guess!'

'With other people?'

'Sure, with other people. Karina's picked out a nice, quiet mare, and she'll put you in with Beginners. Don't worry, lots of guys start here with zilch experience, so you won't stand out in the crowd.'

But Taryn shook her head. It was only Karina striding into the kitchen with a bright 'Hey!' and a high five for Kirstie that took the pressure off.

'C'mon, Taryn!' The wrangler took charge. 'I've got Skylark tacked up ready for you. I want you to ride her around the arena for me before the other guests finish breakfast. That way, you'll get a little practice in before we set out on the trail!'

Karina's high voltage style didn't give the visitor a chance to object. Before Taryn knew it, she was swept out of the house and across the yard towards the corral.

Relieved, Kirstie stared at their backs. Even from a distance and from behind, Taryn looked unhappy through and through. Her slight shoulders slumped and there was no spring in her step.

Jeez, hard work! Kirstie groaned to herself. *I need help!* Then the phone rang.

'Hey, Kirstie!' Lisa's bubbly voice came through loud and clear.

Kirstie grinned. 'Wow, now I believe in telepathy!' she cried. 'You just picked up a message in the ether!'

'What message? What're you sayin'? I just called to ask what's cookin'!'

'Exactly! I'm crying out for help to handle Taryn

23

West, and you pick up the phone! How cool is that!'

'Uh-oh! Hey listen, I'm not a child minder, y'know!'

'Yeah, but if you come on a visit for a couple of days, you can talk to her and make her unwind. You're good at that, Lisa, believe me!'

'Yeah well, flattery will get you nowhere, Kirstie Scott.'

Kirstie was disappointed. 'So you won't do it?'

There was a long silence, then, 'Ha-ha, just kiddin'! Sure, I'll do it.'

'Hey, thanks! But I could kill you too, y'know!'

'Can't take a joke, huh?'

'Only if it's funny. So when will you get here?'

'Let me think. I can most likely fix up a ride out with Grandpa, say about lunchtime.'

'Sounds good to me!' Kirstie relaxed. 'Hey, and then you can fill me in on the whole Taryn story.'

'You mean, you still don't know?'

'Nope. Mom does, but she won't say. I'm still totally in the dark.'

Lisa tutted. 'Well, watch this space!' she cried. 'I'm on my way!'

As Kirstie came off the phone to Lisa, Sandy came in from the porch, where she'd been sitting quietly drinking coffee. She gave her daughter a look of faint disapproval.

'What?' Kirstie protested. 'I didn't say anything that wasn't true, did I? Taryn is real hard work!'

'It's not that,' her mom said. 'It's the fact that you asked Lisa to dish the dirt on the Wests, and, no disrespect intended, we both know what a motor-mouth she can be.'

'But Mom, I need to understand what happened with Taryn's family. Otherwise, how can I relate to her while she's here?' Kirstie explained that she'd lain awake during the night, filling in explanations from her own imagination.

Sandy sighed. 'I'm afraid the truth is probably worse than anything you could make up. And I guess I know that sooner or later you'll get to hear what went on.'

Kirstie offered her mom fresh coffee and sat her down at the table. 'So you'll explain?'

'Yeah, but go easy on your reactions, huh? No OTT gasps and squeals – you never know who's listening in!'

Kirstie agreed that she would sit quietly.

'OK, well you know that Mariah West disappeared on May 28th? It happened during a family fishing trip out to Hermann Lake.'

Sandy paused and Kirstie nodded. 'Yeah, I know the place. It's beyond Marshy Meadows and Dorfmann Lake, real remote.'

'Obviously Sean and Mariah West like plenty of private space.'

'Yeah, like a whole mountainside!' In three years plus of living at Half-Moon Ranch, Kirstie had never once made it out as far as Hermann.

Sandy gave a wry smile. 'Sean and Mariah are fishing nuts. It's the only leisure activity they have. He works practically 24/7 as a Forest Ranger up at Marlowe County, while she stays home to school Taryn.

'So anyways, halfway through the day out, Taryn decides to go back to the car for a book. She has to walk maybe a mile through the forest, then back again. She's away just under forty-five minutes. When she gets back, her dad has thrown down his fishing rod and is running away from the lake towards her. He's yelling at her to get back to the car and use his radio to bring help, that her mom has fallen into the lake and disappeared below the surface, and that they need an ambulance, a doctor, divers, whatever.'

Kirstie pictured the scene and shuddered. 'Couldn't Mariah West swim?' she asked.

Sandy nodded. 'That's the weird bit. Mariah was

extremely fit. Her school friends recall that she won swimming medals. So how come she gets into difficulties in a smooth lake in good weather conditions?'

'Did they find the body?'

'No. There was a big search. The press got in on the act and started speculating. The finger of suspicion turned towards the only other person on the scene, namely Taryn's father. It got worse when Sean West went on the news channel and appealed for information or witnesses who might help the police. The fact is, he didn't come across like a guy whose wife has just drowned in mysterious circumstances.'

'What d'you mean exactly?' As the raw facts hit her, Kirstie placed where she'd been on May 28th and why the real life drama had mainly passed her by. That weekend, she and Karina had been part of the team that Brad had taken up to New Jersey for the reining championship.

'He was too calm for most people's liking. While he accepted the probability that his wife had drowned, he put out the remote chance that she'd somehow struggled to the shore and might have survived. In which case, he was talking abduction by a third party, or else a loss of memory from a blow on the head, which would've made Mariah wander off into the forest without any recollection of who she was or what she was doing there.'

'Jeez!' Kirstie allowed one small expression of amazement escape her lips. 'What're you sayin'? That the cops didn't believe him and began to suspect something even worse? That Sean West actually killed his own wife?'

Sandy shrugged. 'Maybe not the police, but certainly the press. There were articles implying that West's story didn't hang together, and that during the time he sent Taryn back to the car a second time, he had the chance to dispose of a body if necessary. And why weren't his clothes wet when he ran towards his daughter yelling for help? Didn't he jump in the lake and try to rescue his wife from drowning, and so on!'

'And d'you think Taryn realises that the newspapers suspected her dad of killing her mom?' Kirstie asked. The gruesome story was really getting to her, and now she felt a strong sympathy for whatever kind of anti-social behaviour their guest was currently displaying.

Another shrug from Sandy showed that it was impossible to say. 'But I ought to tell you the main piece of evidence that did in the end draw the police's attention after they'd examined the Wests' Forest Ranger Jeep. It came up in the press about a week after Mariah disappeared, and it was the fact that a check of the equipment which Sean West routinely carried in the Jeep revealed an important missing item.'

'Which was . . . ?' Kirstie whispered.

'A shotgun,' Sandy answered. 'And as far as I know, Sean never came up with any decent explanation of why the gun wasn't there. Which, when you think about it, paints a pretty grim picture of what might have gone on out there at Hermann Lake!'

The morning routine out in the corral went on as usual. The groups of trail-riders left with the wranglers, riding in a long procession along Five Mile Creek and Coyote trails. The riders were a colourful bunch in their bright red neckerchiefs and cowboy shirts, with their broad-brimmed stetsons worn low to protect them from the sun.

But Kirstie's mood was gloomy despite this. As she made her way towards the tack-room to link up with Hadley and help him with the chores, she found she couldn't shake off the effects of the Wests' tragic and mysterious story. It wasn't the sort of thing you heard and then dismissed, and to be honest, not the kind of situation that made Kirstie want to say wow! and gossip over.

Instead, it gave her a strong urge to help Taryn. If only she could work out a way of making her relax and chill out while she was here. But it would mean getting through some pretty tough defences first.

Thinking this, walking head down towards the by now empty corral, Kirstie pictured Taryn slouched in the saddle, letting Skylark amble along at the end of the line, with the other kids yee-hahing and having a good time up ahead. But then she looked up to see a solitary horse still tied to the rail and soon made out Skylark's dark mane and tail and her gently nodding head. All tacked up, but without a rider, the little mare took a snooze until someone came along and untacked her.

Kirstie felt a small jolt of disappointment. If Karina couldn't persuade Taryn to lighten up and join in with the group, then no one could.

And where had their guest gotten to if she hadn't ridden out with the beginners? Kirstie thought she'd better take a look around, beginning with the tack-room itself.

'You seen Taryn?' she asked Hadley after she poked her head around the door.

The old man was replacing worn leather straps

on the bits and bridles that hung from the wall. 'Taryn who?' he grunted.

'Taryn West, the kid who's staying in the house with us.'

'The quiet one, huh? Last time I saw her, she was headin' for the row stalls.' Hadley's gnarled fingers didn't stop work as he spoke. 'Seems like a little girl you should take care of,' he commented.

'Yeah. Don't you know who she is?' Kirstie asked, looking over her shoulder at the empty stalls beyond the corral.

'Nope, and I don't wanna know.' Hadley was the quiet type himself, and knew the value of silence. He minded his business and expected other folks to mind theirs.

So Kirstie set off with a sigh in search of Taryn. She passed Skylark waiting sleepily in the corral, then slid through the partly-open metal gate leading to the row of stalls where the farrier would work or the wranglers would boost the food supply of the hardest worked horses. Ben called it the 'Breakfast Club', and among the skinny horses needing feeding this morning, Kirstie spotted Jethro Junior and Jitterbug.

'Hey, Jethro,' she murmured, slipping into the narrow stall to see how he was doing.

The dark bay gelding raised his head from the

manger to give her a small nudge with his nose.

'Lucky old you!' she smiled. 'What's the betting it was Hadley who put you on the list!'

Jethro was the old man's sale barn bargain, a horse whom Hadley would defend with his life.

Moving along, she glanced in at Jitterbug, a dainty sorrel mare who sure looked as if she needed feeding up. 'They been working you hard, huh?' Kirstie whispered sympathetically before passing down the row.

'Hey, Lucky!' she called to her own beautiful palomino, making a mental note to thank Ben for allowing him this treat. 'Are we gonna ride out together, once Lisa gets here?' Lucky turned his head, ears pricked, ready to go.

'Yeah, I guess we are!' Kirstie laughed.

Then a movement from the stall at the very end of the row attracted her attention. She spied the newcomer, Diamond Charm, recognising her by the bright white star. Obviously Ben had decided that extra feed would help her settle in. Also, keeping her at a distance from the oldtimers like Lucky.

Kirstie moseyed on down, almost forgetting that her errand was to find Taryn. So it was a surprise to see from ten paces or so that the girl was in Diamond Charm's stall.

Kirstie stopped in her tracks. Taryn's back was towards Kirstie and it seemed she hadn't noticed her. She leaned against the side bars of the stall, close to the mare's head, gently stroking her neck. Diamond Charm was ignoring the feed and had her head turned towards the girl.

The picture struck Kirstie as something special. Their two heads were in close contact, Taryn's dark hair against the rich sorrel of Diamond Charm. The atmosphere was peaceful, each breathing in the scent of the other, unaware of anything else around them.

So she planned to let them be, turning quietly away. Her boot crunched on the dirt and Diamond Charm looked up. Taryn started, then followed the direction of the horse's gaze.

'Sorry, I didn't mean to break you two up,' Kirstie mumbled. Taryn dropped her gaze. Behind her, Diamond Charm nuzzled her shoulder.

Kirstie found herself struggling for something to say. 'You like our new arrival, huh?' she murmured, without really expecting an answer.

'Yeah, I do,' came the reply. 'I like her a lot.'

Kirstie looked hard at Taryn, who had raised her head at last. And to her astonishment, she made out that the poor kid's lips were trembling, and that her eyes were wet with tears.

3

'I didn't handle it well,' Kirstie confessed to Lisa, who had showed up as promised around lunchtime.

At the first chance she'd got, she'd described the moment in the row stalls when she'd realised that Taryn's emotions were all raw and tangled. 'I really thought she was gonna cry out loud. I should've let her do it, I guess, because it's good to get that sort of stuff out in the open. But instead, I kinda coughed and chickened out.'

'I don't blame you,' Lisa said. The two girls watched Lisa's grandpa, Lennie Goodman, talking with Sandy Scott in the yard. Taryn was sitting quietly on the porch swing, wrapped up again in her own little world.

'Yeah, but it was the first time she'd opened up. Maybe this sounds real cheesy, Lisa, but I figure it has something to do with the fact that Taryn overheard Matt sayin' that Diamond Charm lost her mom when she was six weeks old, so now she kinda identifies with the mare.'

'Could be.' Lisa thought for a while. 'How would it be if we asked your mom if Diamond Charm could be Taryn's horse during her visit?'

Kirstie nodded. 'Let's try!'

So the two girls went to join the adults, putting on their best manners and waiting for a pause in the conversation.

'So things are good up at Lone Elm,' Lennie was saying. 'Seems like a lot of folks want to spend vacation time in the Meltwater Mountains this year.'

'Yeah, we're busy here too, thank goodness.' Sandy noticed Kirstie and Lisa hovering nearby. 'Uh-oh, why do I feel a favour comin' on?' she grinned.

'Not a favour for us!' Lisa jumped in with both feet. 'But we just had this great idea that Taryn could ride Diamond Charm. Kirstie's convinced that the two of them would get along real well.'

'Hmm.' Sandy folded her arms and glanced into

the arena where the new arrival from the Triple X had been installed for the afternoon. The sorrel mare munched steadily on a bunch of alfalfa in the feed rack that Ben and Hadley had wheeled in. 'I need to think about that.'

'What's to think about?' Kirstie persisted.

'Nobody's ridden Diamond yet,' Sandy pointed out. 'And there's this rumour that she may get a mite squirly if we're not careful.'

'Well, I could try her out right here in the arena.' If this was the only reason Sandy had against pairing Taryn up with Diamond Charm, Kirstie was sure they could overcome it.

'When?' Sandy looked at her watch.

'Right now!' Kirstie volunteered.

Sandy nodded. 'OK, you've got thirty minutes to convince me!'

So Lisa and Kirstie scrambled to bring a saddle and bridle from the tack-room. They yelled at Taryn to carry a saddle pad out into the arena. 'Come and watch the expert!' Lisa cried. 'This girl is good!'

It was true that Kirstie was in her element. She loved to bond with a new horse, to work out a trust beween herself and the creature based on listening and making sound judgements about when he was ready to accept you. Jokingly, Lisa might call it her 'horse whispering technique', but most ranchers saw this as a modern fad, and knew that the expertise involved went way back to frontier days when a cowboy and his horse lived, worked and ate together out on the wild open plains.

'C'mon!' Lisa encouraged Taryn a second time, as both Sandy and her grandpa drew close to the arena fence. She took the thick saddle blanket from the visitor and hustled her towards them. 'Is it OK if I explain to Taryn what you're doin' in there?' she called to Kirstie.

'Like a running commentary?' Kirstie shrugged. 'I guess. Only, don't expect miracles out here!' Then she turned her concentration on to Diamond Charm, who had watched with caution as Kirstie had slung the tack over the fence rail.

'OK, so Kirstie is in Diamond's attention zone,' Lisa began. 'See how the horse's head is up and her ears are flicked towards her? If there's something she doesn't like, she's ready to take off.'

Slowly Taryn nodded.

'But it's fine at the moment.' Lisa fell silent as Kirstie took up the striped saddle pad and approached the mare.

Kirstie was guessing that Diamond would have no problem with the saddle etcetera. It wouldn't be a case of working for join up and starting from square one. And she was right. The mare allowed her to walk up close and gently lay the pad across her back. A few muscles twitched and Diamond took a step sideways, but nothing more than that. The same with the saddle. She accepted the heavy weight then stood steady as Kirstie tightened the cinch.

'OK so far,' Lisa told Taryn. 'Now we get to see if she's bit-shy!'

Diamond looked hard at the bit and bridle which Kirstie offered to her. She tossed her head a little, then lowered it and let Kirstie slide the cold metal into her mouth.

'No problem!' Lisa breathed, sneaking a look at Taryn, who only had eyes for Diamond Charm. 'Now comes the real big test. Will she let Kirstie up in the saddle, or will she turn squirly on us?'

'What's "squirly" mean?' Taryn asked in a voice only a little above a whisper.

'Y'know, buckin' and stuff. Rearin' up and generally sayin', "get off my back!" '

Kirstie waited a while for the mare to get used to the feel of the tack. She held her on a loose rein, gently stroking her nose with its bright white star, but avoiding the challenge of looking her straight in the eye. 'Yeah, you're real neat!' she murmured, then she moved her hand down Diamond's neck, under her belly and up again along the horse's rump. She repeated this on the other side, still in no rush to move on to the next stage.

'Why did she do both sides?' Taryn asked.

'I dunno.' Lisa turned to Sandy for an explanation.

'Because a horse's brain only lets twenty per cent of the information it receives pass from one side to the other – there's a much bigger split between the two parts of the brain than there is in humans. If you concentrate on one side only, you literally have a half-trained animal!' There was a relaxed smile on Sandy's young-looking face as she watched her daughter work with the mare.

At last Kirstie moved down Diamond's left side and put one foot in the stirrup. She made a fluid, easy movement to swing her leg over the horse and ease herself into the saddle.

Diamond Charm took two or three quick steps forward, then responded to Kirstie's 'Whoa!' and gentle tug on the reins.

'Easy!' Kirstie breathed, then she urged Diamond into a slow walk.

'So where's the problem?' Lisa asked Sandy.

'No problem,' Sandy replied, watching closely as

Kirstie asked for a trot. 'She's a little honey. I like her a lot!'

Lisa grinned at Taryn. 'You see what Kirstie's doin' now – rising out of the saddle with every step? That's called postin' the trot. We'll show you how, don't worry!'

'Try a lope!' Sandy called to Kirstie.

So Kirstie made a kissing sound and urged her horse to move up a gear. She found the long, double beat of Diamond's lope smooth and regular – no head pulling or resistance, just an easy forward-going attitude that was a joy to experience.

'Yeah, good girl!' she breathed. 'Welcome to Half-Moon Ranch!'

Sandy's answer had been a big, happy yes! Sure, Taryn could try riding Diamond Charm in the arena, and if it all worked well, the girls could take to the trails first thing tomorrow morning.

She went off to complete some office work, while Lisa's grandpa said goodbye and drove on up to Lone Elm Trailer Park, which he ran single-handed. This left the three girls to work with the sorrel in the lazy heat of the afternoon sun.

'The aim is to get you up and feelin' comfortable in the saddle,' Lisa explained to Taryn. 'Don't bother about learnin' rules and stuff – do-this-do-that, keep-your-heels-down, head-up, back-straight. Too much brain work gets in the way, OK?'

Taryn nodded. She moved eagerly into position, waiting for Kirstie to give her the go-ahead.

'Whatever you do, don't jerk on the reins,' Kirstie warned. 'That hurts a horse's mouth and makes her want you not to be there. Her reaction to pain is to buck you off, which makes sense from her point of view, doesn't it?'

'Sure.' Taryn swung up into the saddle without a trace of nervousness. She sat deep, with her legs forward and her heels naturally lower than her toes.

'Cool!' Kirstie grinned. 'Now squeeze a little with your legs and ask her to walk forward.'

'It feels like I'm real high up!' Taryn said breathlessly.

'You are. Diamond is around fourteen hands. How does it feel up there?'

'Great!' The girl's eyes were alight with excitement.

'You want to try a trot already?' Lisa encouraged. 'You have to click with your tongue and keep up the pressure with your legs.'

Obeying the instruction, Taryn found that the trot was much harder than the walk. She joggled in the smooth, shiny saddle and threw her weight any which way. 'What am I doing wrong?' she cried.

'You have to rise out of the stirrups in time with Diamond's rhythm!' Kirstie instructed. 'Up-down, up-down – that's right, you got it!'

Patiently Diamond gave her novice rider time to adjust. She seemed to tune into Taryn's frustration and to treat her gently, jogging along in a smooth trot until Taryn had learned to rise to the trot.

'Hey, you're good!' Lisa cried. 'You're a natural, believe me!'

Taryn's pale face was flushed with pleasure. As she came round full circle to where Lisa and Kirstie stood, she said a steady 'Whoa', leaned her weight back and pulled gently on the reins. 'I always wanted to horse-ride!' she confessed, 'ever since I was five years old!'

'And how is it?' Kirstie prompted. 'Is it as good as you thought?'

A wide smile appeared on Taryn's thin face. 'Better!' she insisted. She leaned forward to stroke Diamond Charm's neck. 'Way, way better than I ever dreamed it would be!'

'Wow, what a difference!' Karina muttered under her breath to Kirstie later that evening. She was watching Taryn groom and brush Diamond in the last rays of the sun. Inside the ranch house, supper was on the table, but everyone knew that there was no way of prising their guest away from her beloved horse. 'Talk about a transformation!'

'Yeah, it's great, isn't it?' Kirstie was winding down after a long afternoon's teaching. She felt happy that Taryn really did have a natural gift for horsemanship, and that her feeling for Diamond would grow stronger day by day.

But the pleasant drift into dusk was interrupted by the unexpected arrival of a Jeep, which appeared at the top of the ridge which led down into the secluded valley.

'Who's that?' Kirstie wondered, going off into the house to see if they expected any visitors.

'Bad news,' Lisa reported. 'Your mom just took a call from Sean West to say he was on his way.'

'Taryn's dad?' Immediately Kirstie felt her hackles rise. 'What's he doing here?'

'Visiting his daughter, I guess.' Like Kirstie, Lisa seemed to feel that the visit was an unwelcome one.

'Yeah, and why shouldn't he?' Sandy asked, coming downstairs in a clean blue shirt and with freshly brushed hair.

'Because!' Kirstie protested, trying to suggest a mountain of unspoken reasons in one word.

But Sandy pulled her up short. 'We know nothing about what this guy is going through, OK! All we know is, he lost his wife a while back and meanwhile he's trying his hardest to bring up his girl single-handed. And I for one admire him for that.'

By this time, the Jeep had arrived at the cattleguard and a man in uniform had stepped out. He wore the dark green shirt and khaki trousers of the Forest Rangers, with a badge on his pocket and a broad-brimmed, well-worn white stetson on his head. He was tall and skinny, with a dark moustache.

'You must be Sean!' Sandy went out to greet him with a warm handshake.

Kirstie saw that Taryn had looked up from her task, recognised the visitor and stood stock still.

'Would ya look at that!' Lisa hissed.

Kirstie hushed her and went on observing from the porch.

'Taryn's settled in real well,' Sandy told Mr West. 'A little quiet at first, maybe, but now she's truly finding her feet. Come and see.'

Sean West followed Sandy into the corral. He walked stiffly, hat in hand, looking edgy as hell.

'Hey, look who's here!' Sandy called to Taryn, who had stayed half-hidden behind Diamond Charm.

Reluctantly the girl stepped forward. The glow had vanished from her face, and her brown eyes had lost their light.

'Hello, honey,' Sean said, sounding as edgy as he looked. 'I see you found a friend!'

Taryn frowned and put her arm protectively around Diamond's neck.

'Why, that's good,' he went on. 'What's the horse's name?'

As Taryn gave a terse reply, Lisa whispered again to Kirstie. 'How come he sounds like someone who's rehearsing to be a parent rather than an actual, real-life dad?'

'It's all down to the situation, I guess. I mean, you try to act normal with your kid if you're under suspicion for killing your own wife. How hard would that be?'

Lisa watched Sean West fidget with his hat and scuff the dirt with the toe of his boot. 'To me he's acting like he's actually guilty,' she decided.

But Kirstie wasn't so keen to condemn the guy. 'At least he drove all the way from Marlowe County,' she pointed out. But then, why was he so stiff and formal with Taryn? Why didn't he give her a hug and tell her that everything would work out fine?

* * *

In fact, the whole visit was pretty much a disaster. Sean West never loosened up, even when Sandy invited him into the house for coffee. And not a single smile cracked Taryn's face during the entire time. She was back to the silent, troubled, pre-Diamond kid.

Kirstie was glad when the uncomfortable visit ended. To break the brittle mood, she told Taryn to find a lead-rope and lead Diamond Charm out to Red Fox Meadow.

'Will she be OK with the other horses?' Taryn asked. 'Won't they want to fight her and drive her away?'

'Not now they've had a chance to take a look at her in the arena and the row stalls,' Kirstie explained, slipping the headcollar on to the sorrel mare and handing the rope over to Taryn. 'Go ahead. I'll hold back and watch!'

So she observed closely, seeing the horse and the girl fall into step across the rough wooden bridge leading to the meadow. She tried hard to imagine how Taryn must feel after her dad's brief visit, not turning when Lisa came up alongside her.

'D'you still think he's guilty?' she murmured.

Lisa let a silence develop. 'I hope not, for Taryn's sake.'

'Me too.' There was another long pause. 'But what if he is?'

'And if he is, does Taryn know that he did it?' Lisa wondered.

Kirstie sighed and shook her head. The sun was setting over Eagle's Peak, turning the grey sky red. Taryn and Diamond Charm were by now small, dark figures in the distance. The scene held no answers to the mystery, only a depth of grief that Kirstie herself could not imagine.

4

The plan next morning was for Lisa and Kirstie to ride out with Taryn along Bear Hunt Trail. It would be just the three of them, taking it easy, letting Taryn enjoy her horse and giving Diamond Charm a chance to learn the territory.

'Ah, shucks!' Lisa had taken a call from her grandpa during breakfast. 'There's a crisis up at Lone Elm. A guy with a trailer came off the road near Red Eagle Lodge. They need Grandpa to tow him out of the gulley, so now he's asked me to go and take care of Reception for him.'

'Tough luck,' Kirstie agreed. 'But I guess it's only for a couple of hours. You'll be back by lunchtime, then we can all ride out together this afternoon.'

So, while Lisa took a lift with Hadley up the Jeep track, Kirstie took Taryn out to the meadow, where they picked out Lucky and Diamond Charm to bring them into the corral.

'It's kinda dusty out here.' Kirstie noted the yellow grass and dry ground. The baked earth had cracked and the milling of horses around the feed racks had worn the surface to dust. 'It's time we got some rain.'

A silent Taryn kept her head down.

'The only chance we have of that is if we get a storm,' Kirstie went on. Jeez, now she was talking about the weather to fill the gaps! If only Sean West hadn't paid his visit the night before. Up until then, she felt that she and Taryn had been making progress.

'C'mon, I'll show you how to brush and comb your horse,' she offered now. She led the way with Lucky out of the meadow and across the footbridge, feeling the visitor hang back when she saw that there were still guests and wranglers in the corral. 'It's OK, we'll go into the barn where it's cooler,' she suggested.

Once inside, she showed Taryn how to tether her horse using a slip-knot. 'You don't wanna give her too much rope so she can turn around and nip you while you're working,' she explained. 'You start brushing up around her neck, working backwards like this. You wanna try?'

Taryn nodded. She took the brush and copied Kirstie's technique.

'Hey, you're a fast learner!' Kirstie moved on to Lucky's stall and began to untangle the palomino's long, pale mane. He snorted, as if to say, *Yeah, it's high time you paid me some attention!* 'OK, OK!' Kirstie argued back. 'Lucky thinks he's the centre of the universe!' she kidded. 'He hates me spendin' time with other horses!'

For a while they brushed and combed, raising dust from their horses' coats and listening to the muffled sound of the groups of trail-riders setting off from the corral.

'Easy, boy!' Kirstie steadied Lucky as she lifted a front hoof and dug out small stones with a pick. By now his golden coat was shining and his mane and tail were smooth as silk. 'Now, we've done this a thousand times. You just quit fussin' and stand easy, huh?'

'Why d'you talk to him like that?' Taryn wanted to know. 'He can't understand what you're saying.'

'You hear that, Lucky?' Kirstie pretended to be deeply wounded. 'Taryn thinks you're just some dumb animal!' Peering over the wooden partition, she told her off for hurting Lucky's feelings.

Taryn blushed and gave a little smile.

Yeah! Kirstie grinned to herself. For sure horses were the best thing in the world for breaking down barriers!

'OK, so now we're tacked up and ready to roll!' Kirstie announced.

She and Taryn had led their horses into the corral just as Hadley returned from driving Lisa to Lone Elm. The old man came straight across to check cinches and lengthen Taryn's stirrups.

'You wanna ride like a real cowgirl,' he told her. 'And you see this here saddle horn? You grab this any time you need to. It'll keep you in that saddle come hell or high water!'

Kirstie saw Taryn stiffen and frown, then slowly relax. She even allowed Hadley to help her up into the saddle.

'Thanks,' she mumbled, gathering up her reins.

'Any time,' Hadley told her. 'Hey, do I get to ride with you girls some time soon?'

'Maybe!' Kirstie kidded along. 'But not today. I got something special planned!'

'Tomorrow maybe,' Hadley persisted. 'How about

that, Taryn?' Colouring up, their guest ducked her head and shrugged.

As if a sudden thought had struck him, Hadley made a beeline for the tack-room. 'You wait here!' he instructed.

Kirstie raised her eyebrows. At this rate, they would never leave!

But the old wrangler soon returned, carrying a battered black stetson which Kirstie recognised as Hadley's second-best hat. 'You need this,' he told Taryn. 'Sun's gettin' up. It's gonna be mighty hot!'

Taryn looked doubtfully at Kirstie.

'Take it,' she told her. 'Hadley's right. You'll roast alive without a hat!'

'Hey, and never say a cowboy can't be parted from his John B!' he joked, watching with a critical eye as Taryn put on the bent and dusty stetson. 'Tip it forward, that's good. And mind you don't lose it in the wind, or I'll tan your hide!'

'You're honoured!' Kirstie told Taryn as they rode out at last.

'I am?' From beneath the broad brim Taryn shot her a quizzical glance.

'You bet!' she promised her. 'Hadley never usually lets anyone even touch his hat, let alone wear it!'

* * *

The 'something special' which Kirstie had planned was a ride up Bear Hunt Trail to Angel Rock. It had come to her suddenly that this was a spot which Taryn would love – off the trail and hidden from view. In fact, Angel Rock was so secluded that none of the usual guests even knew it was there.

'You see why we keep it to ourselves?' Kirstie murmured as they made their way through the circle of tall ponderosa pines which ringed the site.

They'd ridden slowly in the increasing heat, breathing in the smell of pine sap, steering between spikes of bright yellow Indian tobacco plants and prickly, vivid pink globe cacti. Diamond Charm had tucked herself in behind Lucky, treading in his footsteps, alert to every new sound, sight and smell.

But now, after an hour's ride along Bear Hunt Overlook and north up the steep mountainside, with Monument Rock in the distance, they had arrived.

Kirstie led the way through the pines into a tight semi-circle of irregularly shaped rocks. To one side, a clear waterfall trickled into a small pool surrounded by white and pink pebbles. Come fall and the first rain and snow, this waterfall would swell to a torrent, drowning the ferns and later sealing the green marsh plants under a layer of

shiny, transparent ice. But now, flowers bloomed in the cool shade, and a carpet of blue columbines spread across the silent clearing. Behind them, the pine trees arched their branches and gave off their sweet, powerful scent.

'Doesn't anyone come here?' Taryn whispered as if she'd entered an empty church.

'Only people who live at Half-Moon Ranch.' Kirstie watched the girl's face open up to the wonder of the place. Her eyes had regained a little of their shine, her mouth was slightly open.

'Why is it called Angel Rock?'

Kirstie pointed to a strange rock formation on the skyline. 'You see that? The wind and the rain has worn away at the granite. Look at it from this angle and you'll see a Christmas angel.'

'With wings coming out to the right?' Taryn twisted and turned her head until she got it. 'Hey, that's neat!'

Kirstie grinned. 'How about we dismount and tie up the horses?'

'Shall we let them drink first?' Taryn pointed to the clear pool.

'Good thinking.' Together they led Lucky and Diamond Charm across the thirty-foot clearing. The horses lowered their heads and noisily sucked up water, disturbing a couple of ground squirrels and making a blue jay squawk from high in one of the trees.

'Hey!' Taryn protested as Diamond pawed at the pool with her front hoof. Shiny, cold droplets of water splashed up on to her jeans and shirt.

'Watch out for Hadley's hat!' Kirstie warned.

Too late. Taryn had jumped sideways, the stetson had caught on a low aspen branch and fallen into the pool. The two girls watched it float, crown up, before Taryn plunged in after it.

'Watch out for the rocks underfoot, they could be slippery!' Kirstie cried again.

Splash! Taryn slid and sat down waist deep in the water. She made a grab for the hat and held it up above her head.

Quickly Kirstie ran to the rescue. 'Give me your hand!' she gasped as the cold water soaked through her boots.

'No. Take the hat from me first!' Taryn held it out while Kirstie leaned forward and grasped it.

Too far! Kirstie fell off balance, waved her arms wildly then toppled in beside Taryn. Now they were both wet, wet, wet! She looked at their guest sitting waist deep in the pool, desperately holding the dripping hat clear. Taryn's shirt was drenched, her dark hair hanging in rats' tails, lips trembling.

Kirstie felt an explosion of laughter rise. It choked her then made her splutter, before she leaned forward in a helpless fit of giggles.

It was either laugh or cry.

Luckily Taryn saw the funny side. Her face too broadened into a grin. Then she was shaking with rising laughter, spluttering alongside Kirstie and stumbling to her feet.

'Hadley will kill me!' she gasped, holding the sorry stetson by the brim. 'Kirstie, what am I gonna do about his precious hat? Seriously, I'm in deep trouble here! Stop laughing, would ya? I really really mean it!'

It was after Kirstie and Taryn had left Angel Rock and were heading for home that Taryn opened up for the first time.

Kirstie had dismounted on Bear Hunt Overlook to check Diamond's cinch. She'd given Taryn the OK to hook her foot back into the stirrup when the conversation had begun.

'I guess you know about my mom?' Taryn sighed, her gaze fixed on the valley below.

'Yeah. I'm sorry, it must be real tough.' Kirstie felt that her words were weak and feeble.

'Most folks read about it. They think Dad murdered her.'

Kirstie stared up at her. She was about to do what she'd done before – just chicken out and say something stupid to change the subject. But there was a new look in Taryn's eyes, as if she trusted Kirstie and really needed to talk. So she steeled herself to tackle it head on. 'What d'you think?'

Taryn shrugged. 'It looks bad for Dad, but I don't think he could do what they're sayin'.' There was a long pause, then she went on in a low, troubled voice. 'Which way is Hermann Lake from here?'

'West past Marshy Meadow and Dorfmann.' Kirstie pointed in the general direction. 'I've never been there, but I hear it's pretty.'

'We went out there for a picnic. It was my birthday. Dad took a day off from work. Mom and me were real happy.'

Kirstie thought of the bunch of hand-made birthday cards in Taryn's closet, but said nothing about it. 'Your hat's dry,' she pointed out. Unhooking it from Taryn's saddle horn, she offered it to her. 'It's hot. You should put it back on.'

Taryn sighed. 'Mom says Dad works too hard. We almost never see him. So when he took time off for my birthday trip to the lake, she was like a little kid, preparing sack lunches and smiling. She hasn't done that lately – I mean, smile. They argue sometimes, when I'm up in my room.'

Kirstie frowned. This was getting way too painful.

'Mom says we should go into Marlowe County more often. She says I need new clothes and I should make friends my own age. He says we're doin' fine the way we are, we don't need other people poking their noses in, askin' questions about my home schoolin' and so on.'

'Sounds like your dad won the argument,' Kirstie said quietly.

'Like always,' Taryn confirmed.

'How about you? You'd like to meet new people, wouldn't you?'

'No, not really. Kids my age are mad for music and fashion and stuff I don't care about.'

There was no answer to this, until Kirstie grasped at the one thing that seemed to have claimed Taryn's interest. 'Yeah, but you'd like to come here again, I guess. Hey, and I'd promise not to talk about the latest crazes, and you could ride Diamond Charm right through fall!'

Taryn glanced down at her with the saddest smile. 'You'd be my first friend?'

'Sure, I'd like that a lot!'

'Me too.'

'So ask your dad if you can come visit again,' Kirstie insisted.

The mention of Sean West broke into Taryn's wistful daydream. 'He needs me back home,' she sighed. 'Now that Mom's gone, I do the chores around the house.'

Kirstie narrowed her eyes. 'How about if my mom asks him for you?'

Quickly Taryn stepped in. 'No. I have to go back. I wish I didn't, believe me. I wish I could stay here with you and Diamond Charm, but I can't!'

'Why not?' Kirstie's heart went out to Taryn as her face crumpled and tears came to her eyes.

'Dad would be mad. I only got to come this time because my doctor said I needed a break.'

'Are you scared of your dad?' Kirstie asked, recalling Sean West's visit and Taryn's wary response.

She gave the slightest of nods and a whispered, 'I guess.' Then she turned Diamond's head away from Kirstie and rode slowly down the hill.

'Kirstie, Lisa, git over here!' Karina cried early that afternoon. The two little Texan kids were playing up in the crowded corral. 'Kirstie, you show Earl Junior how to tie his lead-rope, wouldya? And Lisa,

Michael can't reach his stirrups. You need to throw him up into the saddle for me please!'

The girls had been chilling out in the barn doorway, letting Taryn groom Skylark ready for Lisa to make up a riding trio with her and Kirstie. Kirstie had been wanting to bring Lisa in on the worries she had about Taryn going back home, but so far hadn't found the opportunity. So she'd been quiet and thoughtful, letting Lisa do the talking as usual.

Now though, it was all systems go to get the kids' ride off to a good start. 'Move out of the way, Cornbread!' Lisa cried, almost tripping over the cat as he scooted out of the barn and overtook them.

Meanwhile, Earl Junior was using his lead-rope as a lasso, swinging it around his head and clipping the ear of the young rider next to him.

Earl Senior yelled at his son from the far side of the corral. He startled his own horse, who crowhopped out through the gate, then lit out along Five Mile Creek. Quickly Matt rode to bring the burly man back to the start.

'Michael, stand still!' Lisa was urging.

Young Michael wriggled and squirmed. 'That tickles!' he protested as Lisa tried to hoist him up into the ornate kiddy saddle.

'Up you go!' she cried, pinning him in place by

grabbing hold of his fancy snakeskin boots. 'Now quit wrigglin' and wait in line for Hadley to fix your cinch!' she warned.

At last the kids were ready. 'Give me steer wrestlin' any day!' Karina grunted under her breath as she headed them out through the gate.

Then the adult parties left with Matt and Ben. Lawyers, teachers and advertising executives alike, after three days in the saddle, they dressed and rode like the rough and ready cowboys who had opened up the frontier some hundred and fifty years earlier.

'Yee-hah!' Earl Senior yelled, taking off his tall Texan hat and waving it in the air at Lisa and Kirstie. 'See you guys later!'

Kirstie sagged against the corral fence. 'Give me strength!' she sighed.

'Hey, what are you up to?' Lisa had spotted Skylark amble out into the corral, trailing her lead-rope behind. 'Taryn!' she called into the barn. 'Who taught you to tie a rope?'

'I did!' Kirstie cut in. She picked up the trailing rope and led the bay mare back into the barn.

Inside, it was cool and shady, with a high stack of alfalfa bales to one side and a row of stalls to the other. The pale golden hay gave off a strong, sweet smell.

'Taryn?' Kirstie called, waiting for her eyes to adjust to the gloom. Remembering the morning's incident with the hat, she carried on with the joke. 'It's OK, Hadley's not here. It's safe for you to come out!'

But there was no answer, and the sensation came over her that Taryn was no longer in the stalls grooming horses. In fact, the barn seemed strangely empty. So Kirstie moved quickly down the centre aisle, glancing in at Lucky and expecting to find Diamond Charm in the very next stall.

She stopped dead. 'Lisa!' she yelled over her shoulder. 'Did Diamond follow Skylark out into the corral?'

'Nope!' came the reply.

Kirstie took another look. The sorrel mare's stall was empty, the door swinging open and the tack gone from the hook on the wall. 'Taryn!' she yelled.

She ran the length of the barn to the far end where a small side door led out on to the creek. This door too was open and fresh prints in the dust showed that a horse had recently gone through.

Kirstie braced her arms against the door frame and stared out into the vast expanse of mountains beyond. The narrow valley was bounded by steep, pine-clad slopes leading to mountains that grew higher and barer until their white peaks touched the blue sky. It was a wilderness out there, beyond the Jeep tracks and the trails. Wild country where mountain lions and bears roamed free.

'What happened?' Lisa came running to join Kirstie.

She looked in vain for moving figures – for Taryn riding Diamond Charm along the bank of the creek, or crossing the water and heading north across Pond Meadow. But there was nothing except distant mule deer, keeping to the shade of the pine trees.

'Taryn and Diamond took off,' Kirstie muttered.

'Alone? Without us?' Lisa asked in bewilderment.

'Yeah,' Kirstie sighed. 'Like you say, totally alone. Let's go, Lisa. We have to find them before they have an accident!'

5

'This kid doesn't have a clue!' Lisa declared as she and Kirstie rode Skylark and Lucky out along Five Mile Creek Trail. 'She's eleven years old, doesn't know the territory and has only been on a horse twice in her whole life!'

'Don't tell me!' Kirstie groaned.

The last thirty minutes had been crazy. The second she and Lisa had worked out that Taryn had taken off, they'd run to the house to tell Sandy, only to find a note on the table saying she'd driven into Denver to talk with her banker. She would be back around eight o'clock that evening.

'Then it's down to us to find the kid!' Lisa had

decided. 'So the sooner we get out there lookin', the better chance we have!'

Luckily their horses were standing ready in the barn. All it took was for the girls to saddle them and point them in the direction of Five Mile Creek.

They set off slowly, following the fresh hoofprints across the dusty descent towards the creek, but soon losing them in the tall grass growing by the water.

'Let's suppose she steered Diamond along the bank,' Kirstie muttered, scouting for more prints in the mud. She picked up signs here and there to confirm this theory.

'Yeah, but where the heck is she going?' Lisa looked way ahead to Pond Meadow, where this year's foals and their brood mares quietly grazed.

'If we knew that, we could quit worryin'!' Kirstie pointed out. The hoofprints had disappeared again, so she took a guess that Taryn and Diamond Charm might have crossed the meadow.

The appearance of two riders made the mothers and foals look up. They flicked their ears and swished their tails, the mares standing careful guard over their babies.

'Cute!' Lisa murmured, in spite of the situation. The young ones pranced and danced on skinny legs. They shook their short, tufty tails, peeking from behind the strong bodies of the mares.

Then, from the far corner, an ear-splitting noise started up. Columbine, the noisy little burro, had spotted Skylark and came charging awkwardly across. She ee-aawed in delight, raising her heavy head and skipping and stumbling as she approached.

'Not now, Columbine!' Kirstie warned. She knew that the burro had bonded with Skylark when the mare lost her foal in the snow the previous winter. 'Your momma's too busy to play!'

The little grey donkey wouldn't take no for an answer. She charged up to Skylark and skidded to a halt, nudging hard with her nose and getting under the mare's feet.

'Scoot!' Lisa said.

Skylark herself brushed off the burro's advances with a quick nip on the rump. Startled, Columbine backed off.

'Look at her sweet face!' Lisa grinned. 'See how sorry for herself she is.'

'Skylark will come play later on.' Kirstie broke Lucky into a trot which left the dejected burro far behind. She'd now begun to doubt whether Taryn and Diamond had actually braved the other horses and come this way. Maybe instead they'd stuck to the creek.

'If only we could get inside her head,' she sighed once she and Lisa had come through the gate on to the Jeep track.

Lisa shrugged. 'If you wanna know, I reckon no one in this world can even guess what goes on for Taryn. In fact, I never met anyone so – all alone!'

'You're right.' Sadly Kirstie nodded. 'I'm guessin' that maybe she wanted some time to herself right now and took off without thinking how much hassle it would cause.'

But Lisa disagreed. 'Taryn doesn't do stuff without thinking,' she argued. 'Thinking too much is part of her problem.'

Kirstie looked up ahead to Eagle's Peak. Gradually a frown appeared. 'Huh!' was all she said.

'What does that mean? Kirstie, what's goin' on?'

'Nothing. Forget it.' Kirstie set off along the rough track, then stopped suddenly. 'It was something Taryn asked me this morning, up at Angel Rock.'

Quickly Lisa made Skylark catch up. 'So tell me!'

'She wanted to know how to reach Hermann Lake. I told her it was west, way past Bear Hunt. I didn't think much about it at the time, but now . . .'

'Jeez, you don't suppose she got it into her head to ride out there and take a look!' Lisa gasped.

Kirstie clicked her tongue thoughtfully. 'Maybe

she's never been back since the day her mom disappeared. The whole mystery is eating her away from the inside and she's had no one to talk to. Sure, it's a crazy idea to try and ride out there all alone. But if your mind is fixated on an idea, it doesn't sound so crazy to you!'

'Yeah, maybe she needs to check things out so she can really believe what happened!' Lisa grew convinced that Kirstie was on to something. 'What we gonna do? Head out there as fast as we can?'

'I'm not sure. It's a three-hour ride. Maybe Taryn won't make it that far.'

'So what do we do?'

'We need people searching closer to home as well.'

'So we split up.' Lisa took the point. 'How about I scout hereabouts on Skylark and you go on ahead?'

'Yeah. And pass on the problem to Ben, Matt and Karina if you see them out on the trails. That way, we'll have a whole bunch of people looking!'

Once the plan was made, Kirstie and Lisa quickly went their separate ways.

'You take care, you hear!' Lisa warned.

'Hey, how long have I been riding these trails?' Kirstie replied, more cheerfully than she felt. Looking at it cold, this was needle-in-the-haystack stuff. Still, she felt that Taryn had already had too long a start and she was eager to follow up her theory.

So she and Lucky set off at a trot towards Bear Hunt Overlook and were soon out of sight of the creek and the meadow. Once on the trail, her nerve steadied and her senses grew more alert. Her mind, too, took many things into account.

So OK, Taryn might hope to get as far as Hermann Lake, but she was new to horse-riding and would soon have to slow down. Besides, she could easily lose her way amongst the trees, unless she'd picked on a landmark such as Monument Rock and kept it in her sights. There again, there were deep ravines and huge boulders along the way, which made it impossible to keep landmarks constantly in sight.

One thing Kirstie knew for sure – Taryn West was used to being alone. Most kids would spook at being out here in this vast wilderness without a companion. They would panic and get themselves and their horses into trouble. But not Taryn. Living as she did way out of town, she would be used to the company of coyotes, untroubled even by the presence of bears.

In any case, there was no use second guessing. All Kirstie could do was ride on along the Overlook, glancing briefly into the secret clearing at Angel Rock, then carrying on up to Red Eagle Lodge.

The log cabin belonging to Smiley Gilpin, their

Forest Ranger, was set into the hillside and sheltered by pine trees. High on the hillside, it served as a great look-out spot down towards the ranch and over towards Dorfmann and Hermann Lakes.

And, as she approached, Kirstie found that her luck was in. There was Smiley's Jeep, parked by the side of the cabin, and the ranger himself standing in the doorway to greet her.

'Hey, Kirstie! How're you doin'?'

'I'm doin' great, Smiley, except I lost a guest!'

'Tut! How come you got so careless all of a sudden?' 'The smiling, fair-haired man stepped down to take hold of Lucky's reins and steady him while Kirstie slid from the saddle.

'Well, I didn't lose her exactly. It's more like she lost herself.' Taking off her baseball cap, Kirstie ran a hand through her damp hair.

'Hey, so now they're running away from you folks! They can't stand the pace at Half-Moon Ranch, huh? Maybe you should quit making them enter the barrel race on Fridays!'

'Yeah, but joking apart, I gotta find Taryn West!' Kirstie explained.

The name obviously meant something to Smiley, whose face grew serious. Tethering Lucky to the porch rail, he beckoned Kirstie indoors out of the heat. 'I bumped into Hadley in San Luis yesterday. He told me you had the West kid staying with you. I thought it was mighty kind of your mom to ask her to visit.'

'Yeah, well you know Mom!' Kirstie felt that Smiley had more to say. 'Did you ever meet Sean West?' she asked.

Smiley grunted and nodded. 'He works the territory north of Marlowe County. The guys from all over this range of mountains meet up in Colorado Springs once in a while – more of a social gatherin' than business, if you take my meanin'. Not that West is a sociable type of guy.'

'So you didn't like him?' Kirstie quizzed. She took the glass of cold Coke that Smiley offered and drank it fast.

'I couldn't pass an opinion,' he drawled. 'I got him down as a loner. He don't talk, he don't drink and he don't watch football. None of the guys can find much to say to him.'

'Yeah, but what d'you really think of him?' Kirstie wanted to know. 'I met him two days back, and he sure made the hair at the back of my neck stand up, the way he was with Taryn and all. I bet he's real uptight.'

'You might be right,' Smiley conceded.

'Then there's the rumour that he actually killed his wife.'

'I don't pay that no mind.' The ranger's reply was swift. 'In America, we believe a guy is innocent until proven guilty, and that's the way I like it.'

Kirstie felt the frustration rise. 'Yeah, but *why* is Sean West such a loner? Why doesn't he let his wife go shopping and his kid meet other kids her age? What kind of a guy is that?'

'Not necessarily a killer,' Smiley pointed out. 'Listen, Kirstie, did anyone think to call Sean West and tell him his daughter went missin'?'

She took a deep breath and shook her head. 'Not yet. I wanna ride down to Hermann to take a look first.'

'OK, you go ahead. I'll call our office at Marlowe County and ask for Sean to contact me. It don't seem right to keep the guy in ignorance about his own kid.'

Although she couldn't argue with this, Kirstie felt ill at ease as she remounted Lucky. Her guess was that Sean West would come down heavy on them at Half-Moon Ranch once he realised that they'd let Taryn wander off alone. An angry visit from him later that day was all they needed!

Half wishing that she hadn't stopped off at

Smiley's place, she set off once more. The sun was high in the cloudless sky now, and the heat was building. Most forest animals had taken cover in dense thickets, so there was little movement as she rode west along the ridge with the sun burning down on her back. Occasionally, a ground squirrel would break cover and dart along a fallen trunk, or an invisible jay would cry above her head. Kirstie ignored them and rode on, swaying from certainty to doubt as she explored over and over again her theory that Taryn was headed for Hermann Lake

Better get this over with! she thought. They'd come down from the ridge into the valley where Dorfmann Lake spread out before them. She stretched Lucky into a lope along the water's edge, feeling the strong, smooth movement and watching his mane fly back. On any other day, with the water sparkling in the sun and his hooves thundering, this would have been a perfect moment, she knew.

On past Dorfmann with its fishermen and their long rods cast out over the smooth surface, to a campsite with small log cabins and a couple of Dodge trucks parked under the trees. Kirstie stopped to ask a guy with a shotgun slung across his shoulder if he'd seen another girl ride by on a sorrel horse with a bright white star.

'Sure thing,' he replied.

Kirstie reined Lucky around and trotted close to the man. 'Are you sure?'

'Sure I'm sure. A kid with dark hair, wearing a green plaid shirt?' The hunter wanted Kirstie to know that he had his facts right. 'She headed right on to Hermann, not thirty minutes back.'

OK, so now there was no doubt in Kirstie's mind. Taryn had definitely made it this far and Kirstie's whole theory held good. All she had to do was catch up with the runaway and talk her into coming back to the ranch!

Thanking the guy with the gun, Kirstie urged Lucky on. 'You can rest up soon!' she promised him.

He snorted and gave her every ounce of his energy to reach the second lake in record time.

Hermann was smaller and quieter than Dorfmann. It lay in a steep-sided valley, with only a narrow, level bank running along both shores. There were no trails leading up out of the valley, and aspen trees grew thickly, their silver-white trunks standing close together, their silken green leaves shimmering in the breeze.

Kirstie studied the scene. There was only this one trail linking the two lakes, plus a footpath leading north, with a wooden sign pointing towards a parking area for cars. Across on the far shore a solitary fisherman occupied a small clearing in the trees.

All was still. The sun beat down and created a shimmering heat haze over the distant figure. Kirstie looked and listened with all her might. 'Where is she, Lucky?' she murmured. 'Where's Taryn?'

Almost as if in answer, the palomino raised his head and whinnied sharply. A reply came from a short distance away – two horses letting each other know their whereabouts. Kirstie started. Diamond Charm's whinny had come from the path leading to the car park. 'Taryn!' she yelled. 'It's me, Kirstie!'

But she might have known that the kid wouldn't simply ride out of the shade into the sun. No way was that her style.

'Taryn, answer me!' When she got no reply, Kirstie pressed on. 'Whatever it is you wanna do, I'm here to help!'

She had to duck under a branch to follow the runaway down the narrow path, then steer Lucky beween two aspens. The going underfoot was getting tricky. Ahead, she could hear Diamond snorting and crashing into bushes, and then at last she caught a glimpse of her rich sorrel coat.

'Taryn, hold it!' Kirstie pleaded. This was way too difficult for the horses. Lucky shied at a dark shadow, almost tipping her out of the saddle.

But the girl defied her, kicking Diamond into a trot and forcing her through a thicket of thorn bushes off the main track. The mare resisted, rearing on to her hind legs and twisting sideways.

Kirstie half saw, half guessed what happened next. Taryn must have hung on to the saddle horn the way Hadley had taught her. She stayed in place and charged through the bush, around a boulder and through the undergrowth out of sight.

Then there was a rushing sound of a horse's body crashing through more thorn bushes, a high, frightened whinny and the clash of stirrups against tree trunks.

Kirstie's stomach lurched. She caught a glimpse of Diamond rearing again, of Taryn slipping backwards, arms flung wide, reins flying wildly to either side. Leaping out of the saddle and leaving Lucky standing quietly, she raced on foot towards the spot.

At first she saw only Diamond Charm. She was riderless, her rein caught up in a branch, her sides sweating and heaving in fright. With rolling eyes and flared nostrils she pulled away from Kirstie, who grabbed the tangled rein and released it. 'Take it easy!' she whispered, taking in the surface scratches on the horse's face and neck. 'You're gonna be fine!'

But Diamond Charm was spooked big time. She refused to be led quietly back on to the path, using all her strength to resist, so that in the end, Kirstie had to untie the lead-rope and tether her to the nearest stout aspen trunk. Then at last she could begin to call and look around for Taryn.

'Where are you? Are you hurt?' Her voice seemed to fade into the trees and rocks. She turned and searched again.

Still no answer. But Kirstie spotted a dark object on the ground, half-hidden by a thorn bush. She stooped and picked it up – Hadley's hat. 'Jeez!' she breathed. Then she yelled out loud. 'Taryn, don't you see when guys are tryin' to help you? For heavens' sakes, would you quit playin' hide and seek and tell me you're OK!'

6

Kirstie had to beat her way through the bushes, down to the water's edge. Clutching Hadley's hat in one hand, she stumbled over hidden rocks and knocked clumsily against branches until she stood gazing out over the stretch of golden water. Behind her, Lucky and Diamond whinnied nervously.

'I know you're here, Taryn!' Her voice rang out loud and clear. 'If you don't come out of hidin', I'm gonna ride right back to Red Eagle Lodge and get Smiley to call the Mountain Rescue team! Then we'll all be in deep trouble!'

That ought to do the trick! Kirstie thought, peering

under bushes and around rocks. 'I mean it! I'm gonna bring in the cops!'

After a few seconds there was a movement from behind a boulder and the runaway appeared. She had a bright red mark on her forehead and scratches on her arms. The sleeve of her shirt was ripped. But it was the cowed, hunted look on her face that shocked Kirstie the most.

'It's OK, relax. I'm not gonna call anyone,' she promised. 'I just wanted you to quit foolin' around!'

Still Taryn backed away, stepping into the water and sinking her foot deep into the muddy bed.

'What happened? Are you hurt?' Kirstie reached out as if to rescue her.

Taryn shook her head.

'You took a knock on your head. And hey, you're shakin' from head to foot. C'mon, let me get you out of this mess!'

'Leave me alone!' came the plea.

'And go back to the ranch without you? No way!' Kirstie went ahead and grabbed Taryn's hand. Close to, she saw that the skin on her forehead wasn't broken, but that a big bruise was forming over her right eye. 'You don't argue with tree branches!' she reminded her. 'The aim is to duck and avoid them!'

Coaxing Taryn out of the water, Kirstie managed

to calm her down. 'Hey, and look at Hadley's hat!' She held up the battered object. It had a hoofprint on its brim and the crown was crushed flat. 'Is this any way to treat a guy's secondbest stetson?'

Taryn managed a sheepish grin. 'It fell off when Diamond Charm reared up. I guess I never should've made her leave the track?'

'Right on. She's standin' back there wonderin' what in the world happened!'

The reminder made Taryn rush ahead to the spot where her horse was tethered. By this time, Lucky had made his way through the undergrowth to the same spot and was standing quietly at Diamond's side. Both horses were dark with sweat and still breathing hard. 'Did I scare her bad?' Taryn asked Kirstie, examining the bleeding cuts on the mare's neck and chest.

'Enough to make her want you off her back,' she pointed out. 'But those scratches will soon heal. Maybe I'll get Matt to give her a tetanus booster to keep her clear of infection.'

'Gee, I'm real sorry!' Taryn approached Diamond gently, half expecting her to reject the advance. But the forgiving mare lowered her head and accepted her. 'I feel so bad!'

With the crisis over, Kirstie pummelled Hadley's

hat back into shape. She put a crease back in the crown and jammed it on Taryn's head. 'Here, put this on. We've got a whole lot of ridin' to do before sundown.'

Taryn frowned. 'I haven't had a chance to do what I came to do.'

Kirstie looked hard at the girl's set expression. Her chin jutted out a little and her eyes were narrowed. Once more, she tried the laid-back, jokey style that seemed to break down Taryn's defences. 'Yeah, I was meanin' to ask about that. It's a heck of a long ride just to take a look at the beautiful scenery! What's wrong with the views we get from the ranch?'

Taryn blinked and lowered her head. 'It's not that.'

'So what is it?'

'I needed to come,' she said haltingly, glancing up again as if pleading for Kirstie to understand.

Kirstie nodded. 'OK, I gotcha. So what now?'

With a helpless shrug, Taryn gazed along the lake shore. 'It was a stupid idea, I guess. I felt maybe there was somethin' the cops had missed . . .'

'Like a clue or somethin'?' Kirstie raised her eyebrows. 'It happened a long time ago. I don't reckon there'll be any clues left.'

'Not footprints and stuff. But maybe the gun.'

Kirstie gasped. 'What're you sayin'?'

'The gun that Dad carried in his car. They never found it.' There was a quiver in Taryn's voice. 'It must be here some place.'

Kirstie closed her eyes to think, hearing the rustle of aspen leaves and imagining secret voices whispering among the silver branches. The idea of murder in this quiet place made her flesh crawl. 'But what good would it do if you found the gun?' *Apart from prove that your dad killed your mom*, she told herself silently.

Turning away from the lake, Taryn began to push her foot into the undergrowth at the start of a futile search. 'It might help me find out the truth,' she whispered. 'I need to know what happened!'

'Even if it turns out to be – well, y'know, real bad?'

Taryn nodded miserably. 'I can't stand not knowing if Mom's alive or dead. When I'm home I keep thinkin' she's gonna walk in through the door and say, 'Time for your English lesson, Taryn, honey. Clear the table and take out your books!'

Kirstie breathed in deeply. She couldn't think of a single helpful thing to say.

'Then at night, when I'm in bed, I remember the times she would read to me when I was a little kid. And I miss her.'

'Sure you do,' Kirstie said softly. 'Listen, don't cry.

I'll help you look for the gun!' Anything to ease this terrible ache that the poor kid was suffering.

But as she began to scuffle her boot through the undergrowth, Taryn broke down. 'It was my birthday. We were supposed to have fun, but Mom wasn't feeling too good. Dad said maybe we should cancel the trip. In the end, we got it together and came. It was a real sunny day.'

'What was wrong with your mom?' Kirstie asked, steeling herself for an avalanche of painful memories. 'Was she sick?'

'Some of the time,' Taryn sobbed. 'Some days she stayed in bed and didn't get up.'

Kirstie took this in without comment. 'Come and sit on the rock,' she said, leading Taryn to the water's edge. Lucky and Diamond Charm would be fine grazing among the bushes. 'What happened when you got here with your mom and dad?'

'Dad went fishing.'

'Where exactly?'

Taryn pointed a couple of hundred yards along the bank. 'Mom was sleeping on the grass right here.'

'And you were bored so you went to the car to bring a book?'

'Yeah. Well no, not exactly. Dad yelled at me for throwing pebbles into the lake. He said it sent the fish away, and why didn't I go bring a book and sit and read next to Mom?'

As the picture formed in Kirstie's head, she imagined the forlorn little birthday girl trailing off through the forest, leaving the two adults alone by the lake. The trees would have been fresher, the grass still green. 'What then?' she murmured.

'I did what Dad told me – I brought a book and came back. But it had all gone wrong. He saw me and started yelling for me to go back and radio for help. Mom was in the lake, he couldn't find her, we needed the rescue guys . . .' She trembled and sobbed bitterly. 'I looked and I couldn't see Mom any place!'

'Did your dad go into the water after her?' Kirstie asked gently.

Taryn shook her head. 'He can't swim.'

'And did you hear any . . . thing while you were at the car?' She meant a gunshot, of course. There was a vivid picture in her head of one last violent argument between Sean and Mariah West, a shotgun aimed and fired, a body disposed of in the deep lake, a gun curving through the blue air to land with a splash in water, far out of reach . . .

'No,' Taryn sighed, catching her breath and trying to fight back the tears. 'I didn't see or hear anything.

I wish I had, then the cops could finally find out the truth.'

Yeah, and you could stop hopin' that your mom will tuck you up at night like she used to, Kirstie thought. She put an arm around Taryn's shoulder and let her cry until she was all cried out.

The quiet lake didn't give up its secrets to Kirstie and Taryn, though they searched for an hour or more.

They found plenty of junk – rusted cans, broken glass, even a ring of stones containing ashes and half-burned logs – the remains of someone's illegal camping trip.

'Hunters or fishermen,' Kirstie supposed.

But there was nothing in the undergrowth or along the shore which they could connect up with what had happened to Mariah West.

'Are we ready to head for home?' Kirstie asked at last, taking into account the dipping of the sun towards the west and the fact that they had a three-hour ride back to the ranch.

Taryn sighed and nodded. She dragged her feet towards the small clearing where they had left the horses.

'At least they had a good feed!' Kirstie tried to

lift the mood, checking cinches, then deciding to lead Lucky and Diamond down to the lake where they could take on water before they hit the trail. Taryn stood close by, staring out across the shimmering scene.

A distant rumble of a car engine disturbed the drinking horses. They raised their heads, water dripping from their chins, waiting for the vehicle to draw near.

'That'll be fishermen,' Kirstie decided, handing over Diamond's reins to Taryn and leading the way back to the narrow track. But it was late in the day for fishermen to arrive. 'Or maybe those hunters looking for somewhere to set up camp.'

For sure the car had raced down the Jeep road at high speed, approaching the invisible car parking area with a squeal of tyres and a screech of brakes.

Kirstie turned and saw that Taryn was worried. 'It's OK, we're not doin' anything we shouldn't,' she assured her. 'We're not the litterbugs or the ones lightin' fires in the National Forest!'

Taryn's small mouth stayed screwed up tight. 'Let's go!' she whispered.

So Kirstie helped her up into the saddle then mounted Lucky. To be honest, it would be a relief to leave the place, to let it settle back into its deep silence. She jumped nervously as a car door slammed.

'Kirstie, I wanna go!' Taryn urged. The person in the car was in a hurry, crashing off the trail through bushes to find the most direct route to the lake.

The girls set their horses into a trot in the opposite direction.

'Hold it!' a man's deep voice shouted.

Taryn pulled at Diamond's reins as if she'd been shot in the back. 'That's Dad!' she gasped.

The pain in her mouth made Diamond jerk her head and kick out with her back legs. Taryn plunged forward in the saddle and ended up clutching her horse's neck.

Kirstie wheeled Lucky around. 'You sure?' she hissed. But she didn't need an answer – the guy was still yelling, and now it was, 'Taryn, I told you to wait, you hear!'

'How did he know I was here?' Tears had sprung to Taryn's eyes once more.

Kirstie's thoughts flew back to her meeting with Smiley Gilpin and his intention to make contact with Sean West. Yeah, that explained how it had happened! 'What d'you wanna do, ride on or wait?' she asked.

Taryn seemed paralysed. She stared without

answering in the direction of the voice, her face white with shock.

It quickly grew too late to ride away. Sean West was fast approaching, beating aside the undergrowth and appearing across the track ahead of them. When he saw the two riders, he stood with his legs wide apart, blocking their way.

Kirstie took in the tall, stern, uniformed figure. Sean's face was set in a mask-like expression, giving nothing away. His arms hung by his side, his chest heaved up and down from his sprint through the forest.

Instinctively Kirstie drew Lucky back a couple of paces, bunching into Diamond behind them. Then she braced herself. How come she was sitting here feeling guilty, she wondered. What was there to feel bad about?

'Taryn, are you OK?' West asked after what seemed like an age.

The tone of voice wasn't, 'Honey, are you hurt? Thank God I've found you!', but more like, 'What crazy trick are you playin' on me now?'

She nodded.

'Is there anybody else here with you?'

This time Taryn simply shook her head, as if the power of speech had deserted her.

'What in God's name are you doin'?' he wanted to know, striding towards them, by-passing Lucky and seizing hold of Diamond's reins. 'What happened to your head? Take a look at your shoes – they're covered in mud!'

Kirstie had a gut reaction which made her want to back Lucky into him and send him toppling into the thorn bushes. 'Everything's cool,' she insisted. 'Taryn just took a little fall, that's all.'

Slowly Sean West turned his cold gaze on her. 'When I wanna ask you a question, I'll let you know.'

Kirstie glanced at Taryn and decided not to argue. The kid had withdrawn into herself, like the last time her dad had paid an unexpected visit. Her eyes looked vacant and dark, her breathing was shallow and her hands gripped the reins. Turning back to his daughter, Sean patiently unwrapped the curled fingers one by one. 'Get down,' he said quietly.

Jeez, this was scary! Kirstie decided. A normal guy might rant and rave at his kid for taking off without telling anyone. There would be shouting and tears, then the scene would be over and everyone would be saying sorry and promising that it wouldn't happen again. But not Sean West.

'I said, get down from that saddle, you hear me?' he repeated, without a flicker of feeling in his voice.

'Yessir,' Taryn whispered, sliding to the ground.

'Hey, hold it yourself!' Kirstie lashed out. West was so big and strong, Taryn so small and young. 'What d'you think you're doing?'

'Taking my daughter home,' he told her in his monotonous, don't-mess-with-me tone.

'Home, as in "Half-Moon Ranch"? Or home to Marlowe County?' she demanded.

'What's it to you?' West shot back double-quick. 'Ain't you the people who let my kid get lost in the first place? For all you care, she could be lyin' dead at the bottom of the lake right now!'

His answer stunned Kirstie, but once more she snatched a look at Taryn standing cowed at her father's side and decided to button her lip.

'Taryn, you're comin' with me,' West ordered. 'I'll call Mrs Scott when we get back and tell her thanks, but no thanks. I've had more than enough of her takin' care of you. From now on you stay home with me!'

'But what about Diamond Charm?' Taryn cried faintly.

West cast a scornful glance at the tired and dusty, scratched and sweating sorrel mare. 'What about her?'

'I need to ride her back to Half-Moon Ranch! Or

at least give me time to say goodbye!'

Her father took her by the shoulders and spun her round towards his parked car. 'Forget it!' he said, giving her a poke in the back and propelling her forward. 'Your vacation's over. End of story!'

7

'You mean, you dallied Diamond Charm all the way home!' Lisa sat astride the gate into Red Fox Meadow, looking out at the moonlit creek.

Kirstie recalled the long, sad trek from Hermann Lake, when she'd ridden Lucky and trailed the riderless sorrel on the end of a dally rope. 'It took us four hours,' she admitted. 'But hey, what choice did I have?'

For a while they watched the horses in silence. Lucky and Diamond Charm were putting in some steady eating time, to restore the energy they'd lost during a long day on the trails. Others stood by the creek, lowering their heads to drink. Across the far side, Rodeo Rocky kicked up his heels and began a charge up the slope with Jitterbug and Johnny Mohawk.

'Just for the heck of it!' Hadley's amused grunt caught Kirstie and Lisa off guard. 'Would ya look at that Rocky! You sure can see the buckin' bronc in that stallion!'

'Hadley, don't creep up on a girl that way!' Lisa protested.

He leaned on the gate and studied Diamond Charm. 'I hear she threw her rider,' he commented drily.

'Taryn was way out of line,' Kirstie told him. 'She took Diamond off the trail into a thicket of thorns. Of course the horse is gonna buck her rider off in that situation!'

'Let's hope her dad sees it that way, otherwise it could cost the ranch plenty if he takes your mom to court. Did Matt give the horse a tetanus booster?'

Kirstie nodded. 'He checked her over and couldn't find any major injury.'

'D'you reckon Sean West could really sue Sandy over this accident?' Lisa asked.

Hadley shrugged. 'There's no predictin' what a guy like West will do. He don't play by the same rules as the rest of us.'

As they considered the troubled situation, Kirstie felt the worries crowd in. 'You shoulda seen Taryn's face when he ordered her to go back home. "End of vacation! End of story!" It was like a light had gone off inside her and she was left in the total dark.'

'Yeah, well when you think about exactly what she's going home to . . .' Lisa trailed off.

'And what she was losing,' Kirstie added softly. 'Y'know the only thing that she cared about was Diamond Charm. That kid bonded with the mare the second she clapped eyes on her, like Diamond gave Taryn a reason to get up in the mornin'. Nothing else mattered.'

As if she knew that she was included in the conversation, Diamond Charm left off chewing and came to the gate. She plodded steadily, her white star standing out clearly in the moonlight. When she reached them, she nosed and nudged, peering over the gate as if searching for the missing Taryn.

'I know, she's not here,' Kirstie murmured, letting Diamond snuffle at her hand. She felt the velvety softness of the mare's muzzle and her warm breath on her skin.

'How come Sean West overreacted out there at Hermann Lake?' Lisa wondered. 'He storms in and yells at Taryn, tells her to get in the car, all because she decided to ride out alone.'

Kirstie shook her head. 'He didn't storm. He was real quiet and calm on the surface.'

'But underneath?'

Kirstie sighed. 'Yeah, underneath I'd say he was angry, but he kept it under wraps.'

The guy's a control freak,' Lisa muttered.

'So what you gonna do about it?' Hadley's challenge came out of the blue.

'What d'you mean, "do about it"?' Lisa retorted. 'If a father wants to make his kid's life miserable by cuttin' short her vacation, it's not illegal so far as I know.'

Kirstie looked closely at Hadley. His lined face was half hidden by the brim of his hat, his gnarled hands loosely clasped and resting on the top rail of the gate. 'What're you suggestin'?' she asked.

He took a long time to answer. 'Anyone with a lick of sense can see that there's a mystery to solve, and until it's cleared up, there's gonna be a million whispers and suspicions flyin' around. That means Sean West is gonna clam up big time. He's actin' like the world is agin him because it is. So he tells the world, "Back off!", and that includes folks who try to give a helpin' hand to his kid.'

'Gotcha,' Kirstie mused. 'Hey, you're talkin' as if Sean West is innocent.'

'Am I?' Hadley watched the sinking moon meet the jagged horizon. The silver disc melted slowly into the mountains. 'I never met the guy, but the way I figure it, Marlowe County ain't the kind of town where wife murderers hang out. It's a quiet neck of the woods, a little off the beaten track, for sure. But you talk to Sheriff Francini, and he'll tell you the crime figures up there are zero.'

'So you're *guessin'* West is innocent?' Lisa said. 'But you read about these backwoods families in the newspapers. Weird stuff happens when you live miles from your nearest neighbour!'

'Yeah, and what about the gun?' Kirstie had puzzled long and hard over this. 'Why can't Sean West come up with a reason why it went missin'?'

Hadley shook his head. 'I ain't got no answer. All I'm sayin' is, the kid deserves a break.'

'And you think we can help by diggin' around, askin' the sort of questions that maybe the cops didn't get around to askin'.' Kirstie took his point.

'You seem real concerned over Taryn,' Lisa said, with a teasing light in her green eyes.

Hadley shrugged and stood up straight. He cleared his throat and headed off back to the ranch. 'I want my stetson back,' he grunted. 'I bought that

hat ten years ago at Buckaroos, and it's still got another ten years' life in it!'

'So let's take up where Taryn left off!' Lisa had decided in the middle of the night.

Kirstie had been lying on a bed roll inside a sleeping-bag while her friend took the bed. Neither had been able to sleep. 'Meaning?' she'd muttered. Her own head had been in turmoil ever since Hadley had challenged them to solve the mystery of Mariah West's disappearance.

'Meaning, let's head out to the lake and take a look.'

'I already did that with Taryn,' Kirstie had pointed out.

'And what did you find?'

'Zilch! Zero!' Just a big, silent, secret lake.

'Whatever.' Lisa's stubborn streak had shown itself. 'I still say that's where we should head first thing tomorrow!'

So they'd played it low key in the morning, telling Sandy vague stuff about riding out towards Lone Elm and maybe calling in to see Lisa's grandfather.

'Which wasn't a lie,' Lisa pointed out as they rode Lucky and Diamond Charm north along Bear Hunt. They'd left before the sun gained strength in the east, while Sandy, Matt and the wranglers had been busy in the corral. 'Grandpa knows what goes on in this forest bettr'n most. I figure he'd be a good person to help us pick up the trail!'

'I'm glad Diamond Charm is with us,' Kirstie sighed. She'd been the one to cut the horse out of the ramuda and saddle her up. There were many others they could have chosen for Lisa, but somehow the new sorrel already seemed to be in on the act. And she trod eagerly along the narrow Overlook, recognising landmarks and settling comfortably into the long ride ahead.

'Yeah, maybe her name will bring us luck. Y'know, "charm" as in "lucky charm"!'

'We sure could do with it,' Kirstie agreed. She felt the atmosphere of the pine forest bring a calming effect to her tangled nerves. The trees were tall and strong, their fallen needles made a soft carpet underfoot and their boughs guarded them from the full heat of the summer sun. 'Plus we have Lucky's name on our side too!'

'We're gonna do this!' Lisa promised, her head held high.

The dappled sunlight made her hair shine reddish-brown to match her sorrel mount. Maybe it was the red hair that gave her friend the fiery temperament, Kirstie thought. When Lisa got her mind set on something, there was nothing in this world that would stop her. 'Yeah, and I'm glad you came along for the ride too!' she added with a smile.

'Puh-lease!' Lisa cried, suddenly loping ahead. 'Cut it out, will ya!'

'That's a good-lookin' horse you're ridin'!' Lennie Goodman greeted the girls' arrival with a compliment for Diamond Charm.

'She's on loan from the Triple X,' Kirstie explained.

'Oh yeah, Dwight Lebowski's spread.' Lisa's grandpa held Diamond's reins as Lisa dismounted. He'd come out of his office at the trailer park with his silver-rimmed glasses perched on top of his bald head. A broad smile told them that he was glad as ever to see them.

'We came to pick your brains over the Mariah West affair.' Lisa jumped straight in. 'You're the oracle round here. You know everythin' and everyone!'

'Hey, don't I get a hug?' Lennie protested. 'And why d'you wanna rake up that old West stuff anyhow?'

Lisa hugged him then stood with hands on hips. 'Maybe it's old stuff to you, Grandpa, but we've seen with our own eyes what's goin' on for Taryn West right now, and it's made us downright determined to sort out the mess.'

'Uh-oh!' Lennie pretended to back off. 'I recognise that look. It's just like the one your mother used to have at your age, and it usually means, "Take cover!" '

'Seriously, Lennie,' Kirstie put in. 'We know the trail's gone cold, but is there anythin' you could tell us about the Wests that might help, apart from the usual stuff about him bein' a loner?'

Lennie tucked his chin back and gave the question some serious thought. 'There ain't much to tell,' he insisted. 'Sean West don't have any family other than his wife and daughter. His folks are both dead, and Sean was an only child.'

'How about Mariah?' Kirstie asked.

'Now, she's different. She belongs to a big family, the Starkeys, livin' out in Montana for the most part, except for her little brother, Joe, who works alongside Sean in the Forestry Department.'

'So Joe is Taryn's uncle.' Kirstie tried to recall whether Taryn had mentioned her mother's brother.

'Yeah, but he's not treated like family by Sean. The two don't get along real well.'

'Surprise!' Lisa's weary sarcasm made them smile. 'Just name me one single person who does get along with Sean West!'

Feeling that they'd just hit another brick wall,

Kirstie had to change tactics. 'Lennie, how about us leavin' Lucky and Diamond Charm in your meadow while you drive us out to Hermann?'

'You wanna take a look at the scene of the crime?' he asked, lowering his glasses on to the bridge of his nose and turning serious.

'I do!' Lisa insisted. 'Kirstie already did it.'

'And it would be much quicker if you drove us there,' Kirstie coaxed.

It didn't take long for Lennie to agree, and for the two horses to be let loose into well watered pasture behind the rows of silver trailers. By eleven o'clock, they were riding in his Jeep past a deserted Red Eagle Lodge, heading on past Dorfmann to reach Hermann Lake by eleven-thirty.

'D'you wanna wait in the car?' Lisa asked Lennie, leaping out as soon as he'd parked in the clearing alongside a white Dodge truck.

'No way!' The old man clambered out after her. 'It's been a while since I set eyes on the lake. But you go ahead. I'll take my time.'

So Lisa and Kirstie ran on, as if five minutes might make some difference to their chances of finding a clue after all these weeks had elapsed. Their feet flew over the ground, following the route Sean West must have taken when he'd intercepted

Taryn and Kirstie the day before, finally arriving at the calm water's edge.

'Y'see, there's nothin' to investigate!' Kirstie was struck once more by the sheer uneventfulness of the place. The mountains soared in every direction, the sun shone on the rippling surface. Some way along the western shore, a solitary figure cast his line into the water and waited for the big catch.

'Wow, it's huge!' Lisa stared across the vast expanse. 'Where do we start?' she gasped, showing that even her gutsy determination was dented.

'Yeah, and what exactly are we lookin' for?' Kirstie felt the same helplessness as yesterday. 'Shouldn't we take a drive to Marlowe County instead, see what we can find out up there?'

But Lisa ignored her. Her eyes were fixed on the lone fisherman, who was having trouble with his line. He was trying to jerk it back out of the water and flick it a second time, but the end seemed to be hooked to an obstacle under the water.

'Hey, Dean!' Lennie arrived and recognised the sportsman. He gave a wave, then laughed at his dilemma. 'Looks like you caught yourself a giant; one to tell the folks back home about after you throw it back!'

The guy signalled dismissively. All the tugging in

the world wasn't about to release his line. He would have to wade in up to the waist and free it by hand. 'Jeez, this water's cold!' he yelled.

Kirstie, Lisa and Lennie wached the small pantomime develop. Dean had left his rod leaning against a rock and was using both arms to balance as he slowly waded out. Once his foot found a deep hollow and he plunged sideways, then, upright once more, his shin made contact with a sharp rock and he yelled out loud.

'How deep is that lake?' Lisa asked.

'Hundreds, maybe thousands of feet,' Lennie told her. 'I remember when they built the dam at the far end in '56. I was twenty years old and worked on the construction for an engineer named Bill Hermann. Finally we flooded a whole town in the valley, church tower and all!'

'Do they open and close the dam to let water in and out?' Kirstie wondered. It seemed strange that man could exert such power over nature.

'Sure. There are underwater currents in there, if that's what you're thinkin',' Lennie confirmed. 'Sometimes we still get pieces of driftwood from the old houses bein' churned around then thrown up to the surface.'

Kirstie frowned. She sure wished the fisherman

would quit messing about in the water. He seemed to be making a big thing of releasing his line, plunging his arms deep, peering down, then dipping in again.

'Hey, Lennie!' He looked up in disbelief, waiting for the ruffled surface to smooth over. Then he peered into the depths once more. 'Would ya look at this!'

'What is it, Dean?' Lennie was walking towards the fisherman, quickening his pace as he drew near.

'Jeez!' A startled cry followed as the man seemed to grab something heavy below the surface. He heaved then dropped the object in dismay.

'What did you find?' Lennie broke into an old man's run, but was soon overtaken by Kirstie and Lisa.

Dean staggered back, splashing water over himself, hurrying towards the shore. He turned to the newcomers, his face white and stretched into an expression of horror. 'There's a body out there!' he gasped. 'I swear to God, Lennie, I felt an arm. There was a woman's long hair wrapped around my wrist. If you don't believe me, go take a look!'

8

'So much for Diamond Charm bringing us luck!' Kirstie sat gloomily at the supper table that evening, surrounded by a bunch of similarly anxious faces.

News about the body in the lake had spread like a forest fire, leaping from Dean Angelou's gruesome discovery in the isolated spot to Smiley Gilpin at Red Eagle Lodge, the cops in Marlowe County, and from there to every single citizen within a fifty-mile radius.

'Did you hear, they found Mariah West in Hermann Lake!' The grain of suspicion swelled to a certainty before the muddled facts hit Marlowe County Main Street.

Kirstie and Lisa were amazed by two things: the wildfire speed of whisper and rumour, beside the sluggish crawl of police procedure. So that while Mariah's death and the discovery of her corpse was being chewed over in the Do-Nut Store and McDonald's Drive-Thru, the cops were still poring over the scene of the crime, waiting for forensics, interviewing witnesses and making a long and laborious record of the day's events.

Lennie, Kirstie and Lisa had been forced to wait at the lakeside, watching police divers arrive to investigate the position of the corpse before it was finally lifted from the water.

'What a way to end a day's fishing!' Dean Angelou had complained to Lennie. He didn't mean to be heartless, but he needed to get the event into some kind of manageable perspective. 'My wife and kids ain't gonna believe the reason why I'm late for supper!'

'They'd better believe it!' Lennie had commented grimly.

The girls themselves had stayed silent throughout the ordeal. They'd answered the official questions with straight yesses or nos, feeling hollow and numb, asking only to be allowed to return to Lennie's truck while the corpse was actually recovered.

The female detective had been considerate with them and taken their statements out of sight of the police activity.

A few facts had filtered through – the corpse was definitely female, it had been submerged in the water for many weeks, identification was difficult and would have to be confirmed in the lab.

Then, at last, some five hours after the discovery, the witnesses had been released. Lennie had driven the girls straight back to the ranch, where Lisa's mum, Bonnie, was already waiting with Sandy. There had been no drama in the reunion, only a few quiet words of reassurance.

'Come inside out of the heat,' Sandy had told them. 'I'll fetch you cold drinks while you sit and rest.'

'We left Lucky and Diamond Charm at Lone Elm,' Kirstie had remembered.

'No problem, I'll send Ben and Karina to trailer them back. All you need to think about is resting and getting through this calmly.'

Lisa and Kirstie had been grateful for the kind attention. That evening they'd stayed away from the guests and avoided the gossip as much as possible. Even so, Matt had come to supper with the news that the cops had arrested Sean West and charged him with homicide.

'What about Taryn?' Lisa had asked.

Kirstie had stayed quiet, trying not to imagine the scene at the Wests' house.

'The welfare people will take care of her,' Bonnie had told them with a sigh.

'It would've been better if she'd still been here with us,' Kirstie had murmured. 'We should be takin' care of her, not a bunch of strangers.'

Nobody had denied it, then Kirstie had come in with her comment about Diamond Charm not bringing them luck after all. 'Maybe she did, and maybe it's for the best that the whole thing is solved once and for all,' Bonnie suggested. 'I know if I was that kid, I'd want answers more than anythin'.'

'Yeah, and if Sean West is a killer, it's good that he's been taken away and locked up where he can't do no more harm.' Matt's practical outlook came into play. He stood up and took his hat from its peg. 'Listen, guys, we got horses to feed and water, and a drive out to Lone Elm to make before dark. What d'you say we forget about the Wests and do some work around here for a change?'

His comment broke up the supper gathering, and it was only when they were outside on the porch that Kirstie thought to take a look at Hadley. The old man had sat quiet throughout the meal, eyes narrowed, keeping his thoughts to himself. Now though, he was staring directly at Kirstie as if he had something to say.

'What're you thinkin'?' she urged quietly.

'My mind's fixed on that kid,' he confessed. 'And the fact is, I don't think we got all the answers earlier today.'

'How come?' Lisa elbowed her way into the muttered conversation.

'For instance, did the cops identify the corpse?' Hadley asked. 'Or did folks just jump to a conclusion?'

'They jumped,' Kirstie admitted. 'But it looks like a sure-fire certainty to me.'

'And do we know for a fact that they arrested Sean West on a count of homicide?'

The girls shook their heads.

'So why are we sittin' on our butts instead of diggin' around for more information?' Hadley demanded.

Kirstie stared hard at him. 'Yeah, right!' she agreed. 'Let's meet up at first light tomorrow mornin' and you can drive us up to Marlowe County. At the very least we can find out the latest on what's happened to Taryn!'

* * *

The Wests' place was out of town, along a long, straight dirt track. There was a metal water tank set on wooden stilts at the gateway to the property, and the house beyond was a small but neat log cabin type, with a front porch and a swing.

'Just like a million other homes,' Kirstie remarked, leaning out of the passenger window. Somehow she'd expected it to stand out. But no, the lawn along the front of the cabin was trimmed, the stone chimney stack picked out with white cement, the windows glinting in the morning sun.

Lisa sat between Hadley and Kirstie, shading her eyes and staring at the open door of the house. 'Looks like someone's home,' she muttered nervously.

'So they ain't arrested the guy and taken the kid into care after all,' Hadley pointed out, pulling up some distance away.

'And the place isn't crawlin' with cops,' Kirstie added. She felt the fake normality get to her and make the hairs at the back of her neck stand up. Jeez, was this place neat and tidy! The windows were painted white, the mat at the front door was new and unmarked by dusty feet.

Lisa pointed to the two Forest Ranger Jeeps parked by the side of the small house. 'Sean has a visitor.'

Hadley was speculating that it might be Smiley's vehicle and Kirstie's mouth was rapidly turning dry at the thought of knocking on the door and confronting West, when a figure suddenly burst through the doorway.

There was a yell from inside, then Sean West himself appeared.

The three onlookers stayed in the truck. West was furious with the visitor, who argued back, giving as good as he got.

'This is the last time you come here, Joe!' West shouted. 'You ain't shown up since the day Mariah disappeared, and I don't want you to set foot on my land ever again!'

'You let me see the girl!' the other man cried. 'Otherwise I go to the cops and tell 'em that you're holdin' her hostage!' He tried to muscle his way back through the door, but West shoved him down on to the grass.

'Taryn don't wanna see you!' he bellowed.

'Sure she does! Any kid wants to see her uncle, goddamn you!'

Kirstie started and gasped when she realised the identity of the visitor. 'That's Joe Starkey!' she hissed. 'Mariah's kid brother. Remember your grandpa told us about him, Lisa!'

'Hush up!' Lisa warned. She stayed tuned in to the raging argument.

'I'm warnin' you, Joe! You're trespassin' here. To my mind you're trouble and always have been. Me and Taryn don't want nothin' to do with you!'

Aware now that they had witnesses, Joe Starkey decided to back down. But he threw West a parting shot. 'They're comin' to arrest you any time now, Sean. And I'm Taryn's nearest kin. I plan to take care of her as soon as they put you in gaol, and there won't be a thing you can do about it!'

Saying this, he turned on his heel and strode over to Hadley's truck. 'You're on a hidin' to nothin'. Sean ain't welcomin' visitors, as you can see.'

Hadley grunted. 'You Mariah's kid brother?'

The other nodded.

'Mind if we speak with you? We're from Half-Moon Ranch. We're kinda concerned over Taryn ourselves.'

As the door of the house slammed and Joe Starkey got into his Jeep, Kirstie and Lisa took a last look at the gleaming windows. 'I sure wish we could get a glimpse of Taryn,' Kirstie muttered. 'Just so as to check that she's OK.'

However, there was no sign of the pale, serious face framed by the crudely-cut dark hair.

'Follow me down the track,' Joe Starkey invited. 'Let's talk by the mail box at the gate.'

'So you believe the cops will move in and arrest him soon?' Hadley asked Joe.

They'd found him as good as his word. In fact, Joe Starkey was still boiling over with anger at his brother-in-law, and ready to answer any questions that might show West in a bad light.

'Sure they will,' he confirmed. 'And about time. The guy don't deserve to be walkin' free.'

'It seems you and he ain't never got along,' Hadley commented drily.

'Yeah well, the way he acted with my sister was hard to stomach. "Mariah, do this", "Mariah, do that!" Dress this way, wear your hair the way I want you to. It drove her half crazy.' Joe was leaning against the side of his Jeep as he talked, arms folded, scowling back towards his brother-in-law's house. 'This went on for years, mind, way before Taryn was even born. Then, after they had the girl, it got even worse. "Mariah, *your* kid's cryin' ", "Mariah, clean up the baby's face", tellin' her she was a bad mother and all that stuff.'

'Miserable!' Lisa breathed.

'Taryn said your sister was ill sometimes. Is that

what she meant?' Kirstie asked. She'd come around the front of Joe's car and was studying his face, noting the frown lines, the receding hairline, the bitter and angry expression.

'Her life was hell!' he insisted. 'I ran out of countin' the number of times I told her to grab the kid and run.'

'Yeah, and you have to work alongside this guy,' Hadley sympathized. 'That's pretty tough, huh?'

'Especially now!' Lisa added.

As Kirstie continued to stare, she saw that Joe couldn't keep up his gaze. He lowered his eyes, blinked, then looked way over their heads at the line of trees on the horizon.

Uneasy herself, she shifted her attention to the heaped-up contents of Joe's Jeep. There were ropes and a tarpaulin, various tools for the car engine, old newspapers and a long-handled axe, the type that tree-fellers use. Also, stacked in one corner were two rifles marked with the Forest Rangers' logo.

It was Kirstie's turn to frown. She looked a second time at the guns, then at Joe. Those firearms turned everything she'd thought till now on its head.

'Did Mariah ever try to – er – harm herself?' Hadley asked, trying for a diplomatic tone.

Joe took offence nevertheless. 'What're you sayin'? That my sister jumped in the lake of her own free will? Forget it, mister. Sean West is the guy who carries the can here, and don't you forget it!'

Displeased by the turn of the conversation, and noting that Kirstie was still staring at the contents of his Jeep, he quickly reached inside to pull the tarpaulin over the axe and guns. Then he turned back towards them. 'I gotta go,' he muttered, climbing in and starting the engine. 'And I don't want you guys goin' around talkin' about suicide, OK!'

Hadley nodded and told him to cool it. 'We don't spread rumours, Joe. And we don't always believe them neither.'

But there were no friendly goodbyes, only the roar of the engine and a speedy departure.

'What did we say?' Lisa protested, standing open-mouthed in the road.

Kirstie drew a deep breath. 'Never mind what we said, it's more what we saw!'

Hadley and Lisa gave her a puzzled look. 'What *did* we see?' Lisa asked.

'Two guns stashed away in the back of the car,' Kirstie told them. 'Issued by the Forest Rangers, one per Ranger, as far as I know.'

'And Joe had two?' Lisa checked.

Kirstie nodded. 'One belongin' to him, and the other . . . ?'

'To Sean West!' Lisa's chin hit the floor. 'You mean, Joe Starkey has had the missin' murder weapon hidden in his car all this long time!'

Hadley called at Red Eagle Lodge and checked with Smiley: no way should a Ranger possess more than one standard issue shotgun. Those things were strictly controlled.

'You sure you weren't mistaken?' Smiley asked Kirstie.

'I'm certain,' she insisted. She wished she could get back the nice, neat picture she'd had before of Sean West shooting his wife and throwing the body and the gun into the lake. Horrific though it was, at least that version made sense.

'OK, so Joe Starkey shot his sister and hung on to the murder weapon!' Lisa suggested cynically. 'Like, no way!'

'Or else, Joe stole the gun from Sean's Jeep to confuse the cops.' Kirstie felt a new theory dimly begin to form inside her head. 'Joe has some reason for wanting to incriminate Sean.'

'Well, he sure don't like his brother-in-law, and

117

vice versa,' Lisa pointed out. 'We've just seen that with our own eyes.'

'But where would that leave Mariah West in all this?' Hadley wondered. 'Did Sean shoot her, or did Joe?'

'Or neither,' Kirstie cut in, suddenly remembering a curious fact. 'Taryn told me she never heard a gunshot.'

'Hold it, guys!' Smiley had been conversing with them from the porch of his lodge, but now the phone rang and he had to disappear inside. 'No more detective stuff until I get back, OK!'

Kirstie, Lisa and Hadley waited outside in silence until Smiley reappeared.

'It's your mom,' he told Kirstie. 'She's ringing around, needing to speak urgently with you.'

Kirstie shot indoors and picked up the phone.

'Why didn't you tell me where you and Lisa were headed?' Sandy demanded. 'You know not to leave without tellin' me.'

'Sorry, Mom, I forgot. We lit out with Hadley before breakfast. Why, is somethin' wrong?'

Sandy sighed. 'Are you ridin' or in the truck?'

'In the truck. What happened?' Kirstie felt alarm bells ring. Surely her mom would have spotted Lucky out in the meadow and would know that

Kirstie hadn't taken him out on the trails.

'The horses got out of Red Fox,' Sandy told her. 'The gate was open and around a dozen of 'em escaped down by the creek. I rounded 'em up single-handed because Matt, Karina and Ben were out with their groups.'

'Are they all OK?' Kirstie asked, holding her breath for the reply.

'All the ones I got back are fine.' Sandy paused before she delivered the really bad news.

'You mean some are still missin'?'

'Yeah, two. That's why I hoped you and Lisa had ridden out.'

'Which ones?' Kirstie asked, though she'd put two and two together before Sandy had time to tell her the names.

'It's Lucky and Diamond Charm. I looked everywhere, and they got clean away. To tell you the truth, honey, I haven't the least clue where they went, so I guess you girls should get right back here and help me look!'

9

The midday heat was stifling. No breeze came off the Meltwater Range, and the sun was a fierce golden globe in the blue sky. A search under these conditions was exhausting – even an hour under the high sun could cause serious dehydration problems, so Sandy ordered everyone to take a water bottle and to make sure that their heads were well protected.

'Did you call Dwight Lebowski and tell him his mare is missin'?' Matt asked her abruptly. 'Y'know, this could turn out to be an expensive mistake if we have to pay him out for a well trained cuttin' and ropin' horse!'

'Quit looking at the gloomy side!' Sandy told him. 'We've asked all the guests to search for Lucky and Diamond Charm when they ride out on the trails this afternoon. Plus you, Ben and Karina. And then there's me, Kirstie, Lisa and Hadley. Sooner or later we're bound to track 'em down.'

'Yeah, and Lucky knows his way around,' Lisa pointed out. 'There's not a square inch of ranch territory that's a problem for him.'

So they delayed making the phone call to the Triple X and set off in half-a-dozen different directions, all under orders from Sandy.

'Gee, this is like a scene from a movie!' Earl Liston, the tall Texan declared. He and his two boys set off with Karina for Eden Lake, along Five Mile Creek and out into the mountains. There was excitement in the air, each guest determined to spot the runaways and claim the glory of bringing them back home.

But Kirstie was too troubled to share their sense of adventure. After she'd watched Ben take his group of beginners out along Coyote Trail and Matt head out to Miners' Ridge and Dead Man's Canyon, she took a two-way radio from her mom. 'Is it OK if Lisa and I make for Marshy Meadow?' she asked. 'There's plenty of good grazin' out there, even at this time of year. I reckon if Lucky wants a tasty feed, that's where he'll head.'

'Good thinking.' Sandy was preoccupied with the logistics of sending so many riders out searching. 'And I guess wherever Lucky is, we'll find Diamond Charm close by. I can't imagine her takin' off solo.'

'No way,' Kirstie agreed. 'No horse can stand bein' alone out in the wild. It leaves them wide open to attack.' Then she tried hard to convince herself that the search would be successful. 'Anyways, even if we don't find them ourselves, they're gonna surrender come sundown.'

'How d'you figure that?' Lisa had saddled up Johnny Mohawk and was ready to ride.

'A hungry horse heads for home!' Kirstie declared. She was easing herself on to Hollywood Princess, the gorgeous-looking Albino horse with pretty Arab features.

'Hey, don't forget your hat!' Lisa reminded her.

Kirstie ran to the tack-room and jammed her stetson on to her fair head.

Then they were off, with the afternoon ahead of them, and a lot of territory to cover.

'Do we know who let the horses out?' Lisa asked, after they'd ridden for twenty minutes in silence.

They'd risen above the first band of ponderosa pines which fringed the valley, on to a high, bare ridge which gave them a good lookout over the next section of sweeping, dipping mountains. Mule deer had scattered across their track, taking flight with their characteristic skipping, kicking, bounding motion. A solitary coyote had stopped twenty yards from where they passed, tongue lolling in the heat, head hanging low.

'Mom couldn't figure it out.' Kirstie paused to lift her hat and wipe her brow. 'Ben was one hundred per cent sure that he'd bolted the gate after he'd brought the horses in from the meadow

this morning. And he's not the kind of guy to make a mistake about that.'

As Lisa sidled up alongside, Johnny Mohawk took the chance to reach out and nip Hollywood Princess on the butt. The hot-tempered mare gave him a good kick with her hind foot.

'Yeah, and that serves you right!' Lisa muttered, reining the stallion back. 'So do we have any Houdini horses who can slide bolts and open gates with their teeth?'

'Steamboat Charlie could do that,' Kirstie recalled with a faint smile. He was the strong black Percheron who had gone back to The Flying U and Don and Rochelle Wilson. 'But since he left, the meadow has been totally secure.'

Lisa gazed down into the next valley. 'So someone opened it deliberately,' she said quietly. 'Person or persons unknown!'

Nothing! Two miles upstream from the ranch, Marshy Meadow stretched out lush and green. The valley was wide and open, dotted with aspens, with a clear stream running through it.

Kirstie took a long drink from her water bottle. She and Lisa had ridden in and out, around and down almost every draw in the valley. They'd pushed through thick willows growing on the banks of the creek, concentrating on the hidden, shady areas where a grazing animal might hang out.

'Twenty-three cows and twenty calves!' Lisa sighed. She continued the headcount with, 'Eighteen mule deer, one coyote, tracks of two more. Signs of a bear with three cubs.' But not a single horseshoe print in the dry dust or the soft mud by the creek.

'Let's try Deadwood Cemetery,' Kirstie suggested wearily. It was the final draw before Marshy Meadow closed down into a ravine which led in the end to Shady River, running in turn into the great South Platte.

So they eased Hollywood and Johnny Mohawk between steep, rocky cliffs to the top of the draw and a high log-jam of decaying pine trunks, dumped there when Shady River had flooded its banks way back.

'As Hadley would say, no horse with a lick of sense would come this way!' Lisa sighed. The rocks were bare, the bottom of the ravine dry and dusty. Towering over their heads, the huge log-jam looked unsteady.

'Let's go.' Kirstie was hot and thirsty. She was also convinced that Lucky and Diamond Charm had chosen another route for their day-trip.

They began the long haul back, taking note of the black-and-white cows, heads down, munching steadily.

'Who'd ever think I'd spend a day like this, checking on cowpats, hopin' that suddenly we're gonna find some horse manure instead!' Lisa grumbled.

It made Kirstie smile again. 'Don't you wish you were in town with an ice-cold Coke, chillin' out with the kids from school!'

'No, really!' Lisa protested. 'I just love gettin' scratched and sunburned on a wild goose chase!'

They joked and teased to pass the time, letting Hollywood and Johnny take their own time to plod up the steep hills and half-slide, half-walk down the far side. The horses' slow, swaying gait was hypnotic in the heat, dust rose in thick clouds, blue jays clattered from branch to branch.

Eventually, they made their way back to their home valley, pausing on the ridge to view the red roofs of the ranch house and cabins nestled in amongst the pine trees.

'From here you'd never guess the mess we're in down there,' Kirstie sighed. 'Two horses missin', a corpse in the lake, a kid taken into care . . .'

Lisa cocked her head to one side. 'Yeah, poor Taryn!'

Two horses missing – a phantom gate opener – a kid who loved one of the horses to bits – who hadn't even been given time to say goodbye. Kirstie revolved these apparently unconnected facts. 'Y'know, I didn't see Taryn when we visited the Wests' place this morning,' she said with a frown.

'Me neither.' Lisa glanced at Kirstie's shaded face. 'I guess she was keepin' out of the way of the fight between her father and her uncle.'

'Or else she wasn't there at all,' Kirstie suggested.

'Where else would she be?'

Kirstie gazed down into the quiet valley. 'Maybe makin' her way back here to Half-Moon Ranch to find Diamond Charm. Y'know, that horse means more to her than anythin' else in this world!'

'You're just guessin'!' Lisa protested.

Kirstie had set off at a trot towards the ranch. Following in her wake, Lisa ate and breathed dust.

'How would the kid get here, all the way from Marlowe County? Why wouldn't Sean West raise the alarm if she'd gone missin'?'

Kirstie didn't know the answers. 'At least it's a

theory!' she yelled over her shoulder. 'And have you got any better ideas?'

'Think about it!' she told Sandy and Hadley as soon as she and Lisa reached the ranch. 'Say, for instance, Taryn leaves her house at night and walks into Marlowe County. She hides by the gas station, say, then stows away in a truck heading south. She jumps out when it reachs our Shelf-Road. She's on foot again, and it's breakfast time. She hides and watches Ben cut out some of the horses in Red Fox Meadow. She sees that he leaves Diamond Charm behind . . .'

'Whoa!' Sandy warned. 'Let me just make a phone call to see if Sean West is still home.' She left them standing in the yard and ran into the house.

But Kirstie couldn't wait to complete her picture of events. 'OK, so Taryn has got to get close to what she's been missing so much; namely her wonderful sorrel horse. And things are so bad at home, what with her dad about to be arrested and her goin' to live with strangers, that she thinks, *What the heck, I'm gonna open the gate and take Diamond Charm!*'

'She steals her!' Lisa echoed. 'Then carelessly leaves the gate open and lets all the other horses escape?'

Kirstie nodded. She didn't have a shred of evidence, but to her the story hung together.

'So how does Lucky fit in?' Lisa asked.

'Maybe he doesn't,' Hadley cut in, making them turn around to face Five Mile Creek.

There in the distance, an unsaddled horse was making its way towards them. Its dusty coat was a dull gold, its bedraggled mane and tail pale blond.

'Lucky!' Kirstie cried out his name. As she ran to meet him, past the barn, along the side of the creek, she looked out for another horse in his wake. 'Where's Diamond Charm?' she yelled. 'What happened? For goodness sake, Lucky, where have you been?'

The palomino heard her and picked up his pace. He was lame on one front leg and sweating over his withers. Rough burrs and twigs of thornbush were caught in his tail.

Kirstie stopped running and waited for him to reach her. She saw him splash across the shallow creek, churning up waterdrops, then sinking his hooves into the mud. He stumbled up the near bank and made his lopsided way closer and closer.

'What did you do to yourself?' Kirstie murmured. She felt tears spring to her eyes to see her beautiful palomino looking so beat-up and wretched.

He snorted and tossed his head, came right up to her and let her stroke his neck.

But only for a moment. As soon as she'd greeted him, Lucky turned around and trotted a few paces upstream. Then he came back close and repeated the exercise.

'What's he tryin' to say?' Lisa gasped, breathlessly reaching the spot and bending over double. 'And why did he leave Diamond Charm out there all alone? It's gonna be night soon, and the coyotes and mountain lions will move in!'

The mare's not alone, if I'm right about Taryn stealing her, Kirstie thought. She saw that Lucky definitely wanted her to follow, so she set off at a jog beside him.

Behind the girls and the palomino, Hadley had stopped to wait for Sandy, who was running out of the house to join him.

'Hey, wait for me!' Lisa was falling behind Kirstie and Lucky.

'Try to keep us in sight!' Kirstie answered. She laid a hand on Lucky to slow him down, waited until he was almost at a standstill, then vaulted smoothly on to his back. Then she pressed her legs against his sides and urged him on.

She was riding bareback, without reins or even a

headcollar and lead-rope to help her stay on. Yet she managed perfectly, working her whole body into the rhythm of Lucky's smooth lope, loosely clasping his mane with one hand and using her other arm to balance.

They sped along the bank, passing Karina's group of riders as they returned from Eden Lake.

'Did you see Diamond Charm?' Kirstie yelled without slowing Lucky's pace.

'Negative!' Karina shouted back.

'Would you look at that!' one of the guests cried. 'The girl rides like a dream!'

'I reckon Lucky knows somethin'!' Kirstie reported to the wrangler.

'Gotcha! But you take care, you hear!'

Karina's voice was lost in the distance as Kirstie and Lucky raced through the creek and up Bear Hunt Trail. Kirstie leaned forward, holding tight to the tangled mane. 'OK, take it easy,' she breathed in Lucky's ear, afraid that her brave horse would run until he dropped.

Still he pressed on. They reached the Overlook at top speed, then suddenly slowed. The trail was narrow, along a high ridge leading to old silver mine workings which were dominated by the tall finger of Monument Rock. Kirstie felt stray, damp locks of hair stick to her cheek. She brushed them back as Lucky halted, then she took a good look around.

She found nothing unusual at first. Just the same trees overhanging the ridge, a crumbling wooden door that was an entrance to a mine. But Lucky had stopped dead, so there must be something significant for her to see. In fact, he pawed the ground impatiently, as if directing her attention downwards.

So she slid off his back and fell to her knees, warily pushing back the undergrowth near to the mine entrance. Last winter this had been a bear's den, she knew, built up with brushwood to provide a warm shelter during the long white-out. Now though, the bear and her new cubs would be higher up the mountains, above ten thousand feet in their summer territory.

Kirstie heard Lucky stamp. *Look harder!*

She searched on under the bushes until her fingers touched a soft surface. She felt more carefully – the object was domed, with indentations. It was very light. Slowly she pulled it into view.

The shock punched the air out of her. Yet she scrambled to her feet clutching her find. She stared at it and turned it in her hands to make absolutely sure.

'That's Hadley's all right!' she muttered.

The old man's stetson, even more battered than before. Here, in the middle of nowhere. Last seen sitting squarely on Taryn West's head.

Kirstie rode Lucky back to the ranch to show everyone the hat.

'That's bad news,' Lisa sighed as she met up with Kirstie down by the creek. 'Why would Taryn let go of the stetson unless she was in some kind of trouble?'

Reluctantly, Kirstie agreed. 'Maybe Diamond threw her and ran off.'

'*If* Taryn was ridin' her,' Lisa pointed out. 'She wouldn't have a saddle, remember!'

Kirstie nodded, rode on at a walk, then left Lucky with Lisa for her to take him into the barn. 'Get him some alfalfa to eat!' she called as she ran on to the yard.

There she showed Hadley and Sandy what she'd discovered, thanks to Lucky. 'Now we're sure Taryn was here on the ranch today,' she told them.

Sandy said that yes, it was probable. 'I finally reached Sean West on the telephone. He was real defensive at first, then he gave way and admitted that it was true, Taryn had run off.'

'I knew it!' Kirstie cried, clenching her fist tight to steady her reaction. 'What's he been doin' about it, that's what I'd like to know!'

'He got in touch with Joe Starkey for a start,' Sandy went on. 'That was the reason you saw Joe at Sean's place this morning.'

'Joe didn't say nothin',' Hadley cut in, then fell silent again.

Sandy took the stetson from Kirstie. 'Sean spent the rest of the day checking every place he could think of, including Hermann Lake.'

'Did he call the cops?' Kirstie demanded.

Her mom raised her eyebrows. 'The cops called him, as a matter of fact!'

'Gee, what now? Did they arrest him?'

'No. They gave him some interesting information about the corpse they found in the lake. They identified it, and it turns out not to be Mariah West after all.'

Kirstie took a deep breath. 'Not Taryn's mom?' The picture she'd been building up anew shattered into fragments again.

'Uh-huh. DNA tests told them it was a tourist from New York State who'd been visiting Marlowe County last fall. She'd been travelling alone and wasn't reported missing for weeks, which is why the alarm wasn't raised until the trail had gone completely cold.' Sandy allowed herself a weary sigh. 'So you can forget all those rumours about Sean bein' thrown into gaol. Meanwhile, I'm gonna call him again and give him the latest on this stetson situation. My guess is, he'll want to head this way and join in the search.'

10

'Things don't get much more serious, do they?' Lisa stood in line for a flashlight and fresh instructions from Sandy. Her face was strained, her voice subdued.

'Once it gets dark we won't have much hope of finding them,' Kirstie acknowledged. 'And a night out there alone for Taryn and Diamond Charm is exactly what we don't want!'

It was cold under the stars, even in midsummer. And dusk brought out the coyotes. A mountain lion could sit still and quiet on a rock above your head and you wouldn't even know he was there.

'It's gonna be tough.' Lisa looked ahead to a night

without sleep, to rescue helicopters and Jeeps raking their headlights across the silent, dark mountains.

'We have two hours of daylight,' Sandy announced to the crowd of volunteers. They included all the ranch staff, plus the more experienced riders among the guests. 'You should ride out for sixty minutes maximum, then turn around and come back. We don't want you to stay out after dark.'

'Then why the flashlights?' someone asked.

'For use in an emergency, if you lose your way. And remember, your horse has better eyesight at night than you do. Plus, he always knows the way home!' Sandy counted the number of riders about to embark on the search. 'We'll soon have back-up from Smiley and his team, and Sheriff Francini is already on his way out from San Luis. Does anyone have any questions before we begin?'

Karina raised her hand. 'Yes ma'am! What do we do if we find the little girl and there's been an accident? In other words, do we bring her back, or leave her and ride for help?'

'I guess that's for you guys to judge,' Sandy replied. 'If it looks dangerous to move her, wait for a paramedic to arrive.'

Kirstie felt a small shiver run through her. The waiting was getting to her, giving time for the worst outcomes to run riot inside her head.

Then at last her mom gave the word. 'Try to keep another rider in sight at all times!' she ordered. 'You'll be bushwhacking through some rough territory and the light may not be good. So don't take risks and stay safe!'

'C'mon, Gunsmoke!' Kirstie whispered, pressing her blue roan mount into action. Lucky was still resting in the barn with his front leg poulticed to keep down the swelling that had appeared on the lame knee joint. Like most of the riders, including Lisa, she set off along Bear Hunt towards the spot where Taryn's stetson had been found.

'Some posse, huh?' Lisa muttered, above the clip of hooves. Her mount for the evening was Hollywood Princess, who strode on long legs ahead of the smooth, sliding gait of Kirstie's smaller Paso Fino.

The searchers rode hard up the slopes, fanning out through the bushes and keeping Monument Rock in sight as their main landmark. This time, there was none of the earlier excitement, only a sense of grim urgency in everyone's hearts.

As the group split up, Kirstie and Lisa kept a steady course along Bear Hunt Overlook. They were looking for signs that Diamond Charm had carried

Taryn on from the spot where the stetson had been found, but soon discovered that the track was too worn to pick out one set of hooves from another.

'It's no good, we're never gonna work it out,' Lisa sighed. Hollywood lifted her head and whinnied, waiting for a return call from some of the other horses nearby. For a few seconds the shaded hillside was alive with the high-pitched sounds. Kirstie tuned in to their conversations, wondering if one of these calls could be coming from the missing sorrel. She gazed ahead along the ridge, aware that the shadows were already lengthening, feeling a chill creep into the evening air.

So here they were on Bear Hunt Overlook, in an area which the missing girl had visited before. That meant that Taryn had planned to come this way, either leading Diamond Charm with a rope, or riding bareback for the first time in her life. Presumably Lucky had tagged along for the trip, or perhaps to keep a wary eye on the adventurers. Then something had happened, right here on the Overlook – some crisis that had split her palomino up from the runaways and sent him galloping for home.

'What're you thinkin'?' Lisa asked, frustrated by the lack of action. Hollywood pranced and champed at the bit.

'That Taryn knew where she was and had some plan in mind,' Kirstie muttered. She leaned forward in the saddle and stroked Gunsmoke's dappled grey neck. 'She wouldn't just take the horse and run, would she?'

'That depends how desperate she was,' Lisa answered. 'Remember, she believed her dad was about to be arrested for killin' her mom!'

Inwardly Kirstie blamed herslf and the whole of Marlowe County for being so easily swept along on the tide of rumour. *Control freak doesn't equal killer*, she thought bleakly.

'I brought her on my favourite ride the day after she arrived,' she told Lisa. 'Along the Overlook, on up to Smiley's lodge and Angel Rock.'

A helicopter appeared over a ridge to the east, and then another. They were a long way off, but the churning noise of their engines cut into the deep silence.

'Angel Rock,' Kirstie repeated quietly.

The secret place, way off the beaten track, tucked away inside a ring of tall pines, where a waterfall trickled into a small pool and blue columbines carpeted the ground.

Kirstie and Lisa made the Rock in record time, loping

up the hills and taking the descents at a trot. Behind them, above their heads and to either side, the search continued. Within half an hour the girls were weaving in and out of the pines and entering the magic semi-circle of jagged granite. Gunsmoke and Hollywood breathed hard. Their ears were pricked forwards, fixed on something in the clearing.

'Hold it,' Kirstie warned. She reined Gunsmoke back and listened.

A horse called in a shrill whinney from beneath Angel Rock.

'Good job!' Lisa whispered as she realised they were dead on target.

Kirstie nodded. She'd followed her gut feeling and been proved right. 'Hey, Taryn!' she called. 'It's me, Kirstie. Lisa's here too. How're you doin'?'

There was no answer, except for the sound of Diamond Charm's approaching hooves.

The sorrel mare appeared between two pine trees, head up, caught in the last rays of sunlight. She had the look of an animal who had maintained a long vigil – strained and nervous, seeing danger in every shadow.

Kirstie and Lisa dismounted. They approached Diamond on foot, not surprised to see her turn and lead them deep into the clearing, where the sound of water grew louder and the misty blue of the flowers intensified. The shape of the angel towered over them.

The sun had gone from the sheltered spot, and the shade was deep. But there was enough light to make out a small figure slumped against a tree.

The girls ran to Taryn's side and dropped to their knees. Her head lolled forward as if she was asleep, her thick, dark hair hid her face.

'Wake up!' Kirstie urged softly, pushing back the curtain of hair.

They saw Taryn's eyelids flicker. Her lips were dry as she raised her head, so Lisa ran and scooped water from the cool pool into her hat, took it back and used her fingertips to dribble drops into Taryn's mouth.

'Mom, come back, you're too far out!' Taryn whispered, her eyes glazed, her voice high and strained like a small child's.

Lisa drew a sharp breath then tried again with the water.

Taryn licked her lips. 'Mom, the lake's dangerous! Mom!'

'She's hallucinatin'!' Kirstie whispered to Lisa. 'I guess she's got heat stroke – too much sun, not enough to drink.'

'I'll fetch my canteen from my saddle bag, give her a proper drink,' Lisa promised, running off to find Hollywood.

'Taryn, you're on Half-Moon Ranch. There's no lake. Everything's fine!' Kirstie explained.

Taryn's eyes rolled. She tried to focus on the owner of the voice.

'It's me, Kirstie. Everything is gonna work out, you hear!'

'Mom drowned!' she sighed, then sobbed, her mouth dragged down at the corners in a pitiful way. 'Dad didn't try to save her!'

'Hush. Try not to think about it. We've got to get you back home.'

Suddenly Taryn tried to sit up straight. 'No!'

'It's OK, I don't mean "home" home. I'm talkin' about the ranch. We've got half the county out lookin' for you!'

Once more Taryn struggled feebly. She made out Diamond Charm standing guard nearby. 'Mountain lion!' she warned.

Instinctively Kirstie looked over her shoulder. 'No, you're imaginin' things. It's OK.'

'In the bear's den on the ridge – mountain lion – Diamond spooked, I lost my hat.'

'Yeah, OK, I gotcha. But there's no lion here now.

Diamond brought you to a safe place. Lucky came back and raised the alarm.'

Just as Kirstie began to make sense of what had happened with Taryn, Lisa came racing back with more news. 'Hadley's truck was headin' up the Jeep track. I stood on a rock and yelled for him to come. He's on his way!'

So help was nearer at hand than Kirstie had hoped. She knew Hadley would have a radio and that paramedics would reach them before dark.

'I want to stay with Diamond Charm!' Taryn pleaded, catching hold of Kirstie's wrist. Her eyes were large and scared, her grip desperate.

'Don't worry, I'll dally her back home behind Gunsmoke,' Kirstie promised. 'You're sick. You have a fever. You need to go with the ambulance.'

'No, I wanna stay here!' Wildly Taryn pulled away and tried to stand. 'I like it here. Please don't make me go!'

'Taryn, take it easy!' Kirstie felt that the situation was slipping out of control. How did you reason with a person who was half-in, half-out of a nightmare, refusing to face reality?

She was relieved to hear footsteps and to see Hadley's wiry figure appear.

The old man took in the scene – the horse

standing to attention, Kirstie and Lisa pleading with a wild, frantic girl. He strode through the clearing and took charge. 'Hey, Miss!' he said to Taryn, 'what did I tell you was the first cowboy rule?'

She sank back against Diamond Charm, one arm clasped around the horse's neck.

'Huh?' Hadley persisted, gentle as if he was talking to a baby. He came up close, smiling softly, producing a battered stetson from behind his back. 'Rule number one: a cowboy and his John B ain't never parted. Come rain, come shine, this baby stays where it belongs, right here, like this, sittin' plumb on top of your head!'

11

Dusk had fallen and drained the greens and golds out of the hills. The sun had sunk behind Eagle's Peak. Around the ranch house a bustle of cars came and went.

'Taryn is gonna be fine!' Sandy announced from the porch step. 'The doctor diagnosed heat exhaustion. She needs a night's sleep and some TLC, and that'll fix it.'

Tender loving care. Kirstie frowned. What chance of that? She sat with Lisa on the corral fence, watching the crowd disperse.

'Why the serious face?' Lisa asked. 'We did a good job back there!'

'Then why don't I *feel* good?' she moped, dropping down from the fence and wandering towards the barn. 'No, don't spell it out. I already know!'

The problem wasn't with rescuing Taryn. Thanks to Lucky, Diamond Charm and Hadley, that part had run smoothly. But Kirstie couldn't get out of her mind Taryn's face as the paramedics had stretchered her out from under Angel Rock. It had been full of pain and sadness – the face of a kid whose suffering was far from over.

Bones could be mended, fevers doused with medication. But healing loneliness and sorrow was a harder act altogether.

Kirstie's way into the barn to check on Lucky was halted by the approach of yet another car. 'Who now?' she wondered, since by this time the rescue teams were all beginning to disperse, their red tail-lights winding out of the valley along the Shelf-Road.

'That looks like Sean West sitting in the back,' Lisa pointed out. 'And ain't that Joe Starkey with him?'

Kirstie had to look hard to make sure. The two backseat passengers sure looked like the feuding brothers-in-law. But she didn't recognise the guy who was driving the silver Chrysler, nor the muffled figure of the front seat passenger beside him.

'Better late than never,' Lisa muttered. It was many hours since Sandy had called Sean West to inform him that Taryn had taken Diamond Charm and ridden away. 'But it kinda sucks for him not to show up until the crisis is over!'

The two Rangers quickly got out and slammed the doors shut. Sean looked up at the bedroom windows, while Joe went and knocked on the door of the house. He spoke urgently to Sandy.

'I wonder how Taryn's gonna react to a bedside visit.' Like Lisa, Kirstie took a dim view of West's arrival. After all, she'd yet to see Taryn look relaxed and happy in the presence of her strict, control freak father.

The conversation between Sandy and Joe was getting heated. Joe was pointing to the Chrysler and giving a long, complicated explanation. Sean strode impatiently up and down the yard, smoking a cigarette and casting the glowing stub into the dirt.

Kirstie and Lisa approached until they were within earshot.

'Run that by me again,' Sandy said to Joe Starkey. 'I mean, the part about the shotgun.'

'That was my idea,' he confessed. 'I wanted to

make things look real bad for Sean because of what he'd done to my sister. I knew the cops would be pokin' around, makin' him a major suspect, so I figured that if he couldn't produce his regulation weapon for them to examine, that'd put him in a bad light.'

'Yeah, well that worked pretty good,' Sandy confirmed with heavy sarcasm. She shook her head and glanced in the direction of the silver car. 'The whole of Marlowe County was swearing on the Bible that your brother-in-law had killed your sister and thrown the murder weapon into the lake!'

'He learned his lesson, livin' under a cloud of suspicion these last two months,' Starkey said darkly. 'It was a spur of the moment thing, and I always planned to give the gun back. The thing only got out of control yesterday, when that damn fisherman dragged a body out of the water!'

Sandy walked along the wooden porch, her boot heels clicking loudly. 'Didn't you worry about the effect it would have on Taryn, her believin' that her dad had killed her mom, like the rest of us?' she demanded. 'Where was the poor kid in all of this?'

Joe scratched his head, unable to find an answer.

Meanwhile, Lisa turned to Kirstie. 'Am I missin' something here?' she hissed. In this dim light it was impossible to read the expressions on people's faces, or to identify the two mystery people still in the car.

Kirstie shrugged. 'It looks like Joe set Sean up, but now for some reason they've called a truce. Jeez, don't ask me!'

There was a movement of the thin white drapes up at a bedroom window, and a glimpse of Taryn's pale face.

'OK, and what about Sean himself?' Sandy's exasperation with Joe Starkey was growing. 'How cruel was that, to let him go on believing that Mariah had drowned!'

'*Believing* that Mariah had drowned!' This was too much for Kirstie and Lisa to bear without butting in.

'Are you sayin' she didn't really die in the lake?' Lisa demanded, running to intercept Sandy before she stepped down from the porch.

'Come over here,' Sandy told them, striding to the Chrysler and leaning in towards the passenger seat.

Kirstie made out a woman sitting with her jacket collar turned up and her long, black hair tied tightly back. She wore no make-up, there were dark hollows under her eyes and her jaw was clenched tight.

'Meet Mariah West,' Sandy said bluntly. 'And according to what Joe's just told me, this is her therapist, Dr James Cononley.'

'A woman who fakes her own death to escape a bad marriage is seriously ill.' Dr Cononley gave the official medical view. 'She's suffering from a complete mental and emotional breakdown which requires long-term professional treatment, and it's my role to provide that help.'

Kirstie stared at the sick woman. Hadn't Mariah West heard of marriage counsellors? Did she have to plunge under the water and swim out of sight, wait until non-swimmer Sean ran to Taryn for help, then surface behind a rock, wait again until the coast was clear, then make her secret getaway to her kid brother's house?

But then again, it was as Dr Cononley said – Mariah wasn't thinking straight. She'd dreamed up a crazy plan because she was just that – crazy!

'My patient's condition has improved of late,' the doctor assured them. He'd stepped out of the car and left Mariah sitting alone. 'She's emerging from a deep depression and is almost ready to face the consequences of her actions.

'In fact, this is her first trip out of the sanatorium

– a response to Joe's calling earlier today to tell her that Sean was about to be thrown in gaol for her murder. Plus, this would mean that Taryn would effectively become an orphan. This was the first I knew about the actual situation behind Mariah's arrival at the clinic – nobody let me in on her real name and background until today. So, in the circumstances, I agreed with her that she should intervene as soon as possible.

'I drove her to her home in Marlowe County to set the record straight, only to find that there was a new crisis. The child had run away, which did in fact bring the parents together in their desire to find their daughter. So here we are now.'

'Did you know where Mariah was all this time?' Lisa asked Joe Starkey, her eyes wide with astonishment.

Joe bit his lip and nodded. 'I swore not to tell. She came to me for help, and I agreed to drive her out of the state and find her a place to stay. What could I do, she's my sister!'

Kirstie fixed her attention on Sean West. She wanted to feel sorry for him, but all she saw was a tall, unbending figure, a crisp uniform, an expressionless face.

I'd rather be an orphan! she thought miserably.

Then Taryn appeared in the doorway. She'd got dressed in her torn shirt and old jeans, with unlaced trainers on her feet. Sean started when he saw her, then turned to open the car door. Slowly Mariah West got out.

Taryn began to move towards her. She looked like a girl sleepwalking, one hand stretched out in front as if touching was the only way of believing.

'Taryn!' Mariah whispered.

Taryn's fingers made contact with the fabric of her mother's jacket. 'Mom,' she whispered.

'I'm so sorry!'

'Don't be.'

'I'll get better, honey, I promise! We'll be together.'

Taryn nodded. 'Can we live in town? Can I go to school?'

'You bet.'

Kirstie looked again at Sean. The mask wasn't cracking the least bit. The guy hadn't shown a genuine emotion in years and he wasn't about to start now.

'I've agreed to a separation,' he told them. 'It's for the best in the long run.'

'And will you want to take Taryn back while Mariah completes her treatment?' Sandy asked gently. No way was she making judgments here, Kirstie realised. 'Or would you prefer her to stay here at Half-Moon Ranch with us? We'd love to have her if she wants to stay.'

Sean cleared his throat. He blinked and bowed his head. 'I want Taryn to decide that.'

Everyone turned to wait for her decision.

'Are you sure you don't need me to do the chores?' she said haltingly. 'I could come home if you want.'

He took a step forward, then hesitated. 'If you're gonna be happy here, you should stay. I can come visit.'

Kirstie bit her lip and stared. Sean would never let you see it, but he was suffering big time. She'd got him all wrong until that moment when he'd stepped forward to take Taryn back, then stopped himself.

'Then I'll stay here until Mom's better,' Taryn whispered, standing under the first stars of the night, holding tight to her mother's hand.

Everything fell back into silence.

The arrangements were made for Taryn to spend time as part of the family at Half-Moon Ranch. It *was* for the best, they agreed.

'So now I've got a kid sister!' Kirstie sighed. She'd brought Diamond Charm in from the meadow so that Taryn could say goodnight. The mare came willingly, high-stepping across the footbridge into the corral.

'Go ahead!' Lisa invited Taryn to step forward to meet her dream horse. 'Look, she wants to check you out!'

Slowly Taryn went to meet Diamond Charm, who came right up to her and nudged her softly.

'You stayed with me at Angel Rock,' she whispered, putting her arm around her bowed neck.

'That's what horses do,' Kirstie murmured. 'They stick around when you need them.'

She watched the fear melt from Taryn's tense, exhausted body as she stroked the white star on Diamond's forehead. This was where she would find happiness, working with the horses, learning how to trust.

Kirstie looked up at the stars, immeasurably high above her head. The sky was a vast canopy of twinkling lights. She, Lisa, Taryn and Diamond Charm were tiny specks on a big, dark planet.

She took a deep breath, turned to Taryn and smiled.

Nish was winded. He lay where he had fallen when Edward Rose made his spectacular play.

Mr. Dillinger raced out, a water bottle in one hand. He worked on Nish while the rest of the players milled about. The crowd was silent.

Travis figured that, as captain, he should really go over and see how serious it was. He skated over slowly, stick held over the tops of his shin pads, leaning and looking straight down.

Nish was lying there, a huge smile on his face. "Just restin', Trav," he said. "Just give the ol' Nisher another minute and I'll get that goal back."

Mr. Dillinger looked up, his eyes rolling. Finally Nish got to his knees, and a huge roar of appreciation went up from the crowd.

Nish mumbled his ridiculous Elvis impression: "Thank you, thank you very much . . ."

Travis shook his head.

Nish insisted on staying in. He went back to his defence position and crouched, waiting.

Travis looked over at Muck. Muck was staring, blinking, unsure what to say. Sam was on her way off. Muck held up a hand indicating she should stay. He wanted his two top defence in the play.

Edward Rose won the faceoff, but Sarah, coming in from the side, knocked the ball away and it scooted toward Travis.

Travis used his wheels to catch the ball and kick it up onto his stick. He then smartly slipped

it through the skates of the opposing winger and stepped around his check.

Dmitri was waiting for the pass back, hoping, once more, to trap the Young Lions into chasing him as he circled and faded.

But Nish was charging straight up centre! Straight up, like a train, banging his stick as hard as he could.

Travis had been about to send a quick pass to Dmitri. Instead, he used a backhand flip to toss the ball into the centre area, where Nish picked it up at full speed.

Nish broke over centre and faked, sending one defender down on one knee, and then he jumped – high in the air – over the stick of the other defence, the ball rolling through with him.

He landed and shot at the same time.

Travis wondered if he'd ever seen a puck on ice shot so hard.

The ball ripped off Nish's stick, hit the Young Lions' goalie in the shoulder, and popped straight up.

Nish was still coming in. He reached over and deftly ticked the ball out of the air and in behind the falling goaltender, almost crashing through the backboards as he did so.

The crowd exploded! The referee blew his whistle to signal a goal, then again to signal the end of regular time.

Screech Owls 8, Young Lions 8.

Muck and Mr. Dillinger came out onto the floor to join the celebrations – Nish red-faced and delighted at the bottom of a heap of laughing Screech Owls – and then quickly ran over to the opposition bench where they huddled with the coaches and the officials.

The official blew his whistle again. The tie game would stand.

An even larger cheer went up from the crowd when they realized what had been decided.

It seemed the perfect thing to do.

21

THE SCREECH OWLS' AIR CANADA FLIGHT WAS TO leave at ten in the morning. They'd be back in Canada, thanks to the change in time zones, by lunch.

It seemed crazy to Travis. But then, so did everything else about this trip.

The best news was on the front page of the newspaper Mr. Dillinger was waving as he walked into the lobby. The missing ravens, Thor and Cedric, had suddenly reappeared at the Tower of London.

The Crown was secure once more – and the legend of the ravens stronger still after the modern-day Guy Fawkes plot.

All was well, too, with the Screech Owls. The two teams, the Owls and the Young Lions of Wembley, had a party at the hotel the final night, the food and soft drinks provided by New Scotland Yard, the entertainment offered free by the hotel.

The Young Lions had come and joked and even danced, and the next morning the Owls were still laughing and whispering about the fact

that, at some time during the evening, Sam and Sarah and Travis and Edward Rose had gone missing for more than an hour.

Travis at first didn't like the teasing — he couldn't bear to imagine what they might be thinking — but Sam and Sarah laughed it off so well that, after a while, he didn't care either. Certainly it didn't bother Edward Rose, who seemed used to being teased about his effect on girls.

Besides, it was only a matter of minutes before they found out what the four had been up to.

"LADIES AND GENTLEMEN!" SAM ANNOUNCED just as the last of the luggage had been stacked in the lobby for the bus lift to the airport. "We invite you to a special presentation in Ballroom A."

Everyone looked at each other. No one knew what to make of it. The Young Lions, who had come back in the morning to see their new friends off, were as confused as the Screech Owls.

"What's this all about?" Nish demanded, his face a twisted tomato.

"Come see," said Travis.

Travis walked with his best friend all the way to the ballroom. The hotel had been kind enough to let the four of them have the room for as long as they had needed it, and they had even gotten into the spirit of the occasion by supplying much of the necessary material.

There was a sign over the entrance.

MADAME TUSSAUD'S CHAMBER OF HORRORS.

Sam threw the doors open.

There was nothing inside but a single structure

in the centre of the room, with a white tablecloth draped over it and a large sign turned backwards. All the Owls and Lions squeezed into the room, trying to see what the fuss was about. Several tried to get a look at the sign, but Sam wouldn't let them get close enough to see.

"This is bogus!" complained Nish. "What's this all about?"

"You, Big Boy!" Sam happily announced.

"Whaddaya mean, me?" Nish asked, his face clouding with suspicion.

"You said your dream was to have your own spot in Madame Tussaud's, remember?"

"Yeah, so?"

"Well . . ." Sam said, and turned the sign around.

The players stared, some starting to giggle.

The sign said:

WAYNE "NISH" NISHIKAWA
WHO SAVED THE ROYAL FAMILY
FROM THE SECOND GUY FAWKES

Nish brightened up. "Outstanding!" he shouted, clapping his hands together. "Let's see it!"

"You do the honours," said Sam, stepping aside and pulling up a chair so Nish could stand on it and pluck the tablecloth clean off the statue. Nish got up, turned even redder, bowed and yanked the cloth.

It flew off.

Underneath was a full figure of Nish in his complete International In-Line hockey equipment.

Nish's sweater, number 44, with the "A" on the chest, was stuffed with straw, just the way Guy Fawkes was every fifth of November.

The golden helmet was on his head. And inside the oversized helmet, complete with painted eyes and nose, was Sam's treasured tape ball.

"Why did you use that?" Nish asked, exasperated.

"Hey," answered Sam. "You're the guy who said it was *stupid* – remember?"

THE END